PLAYING DIRTY
By A K Love

Playing Dirty

Cover Art: Addendum Designs

To Jodie - my number one fan and the best beta reader a new author could ask for.

DARYL

Nothing prepared me for the sight of her in the flesh. She took my breath away from the moment I walked into the diner a month ago. Her natural beauty instantly drew my gaze and her warmth pulled me to her like a magnet.

She'd seemed nervous that first morning and had spilled coffee all over the table while she was refilling my cup, apologising profusely as she tried to mop it up. Her flush of embarrassment and the tremor of her hands had only increased the instant attraction I felt for her.

On impulse, I'd reached across and placed my hand over hers, stilling her frantic movements. I can still feel the electricity that crackled between us as her green eyes lifted to mine, a mixture of surprise and uncertain desire in them at the physical contact. We'd stayed like that, our gazes locked, until another customer asking for a refill had interrupted the moment, causing Trish to tear her eyes away from mine.

I'd asked her to join me for coffee during her break that first morning. It seemed like the perfect opportunity to set the ball in motion to obtain the information I need. Every morning since, she's joined me during her break and every day my feelings for her have grown.

I keep telling myself that my interest in her is purely professional but the truth is I like being near her. I never imagined how much I would look forward to our time together. I wanted to learn more about her, about the real woman behind the dry facts contained in her file.

The thick folder tells me everything I need to know about her on a professional level but it doesn't reveal the real essence of the woman, what makes her tick. The flat and grainy photographs it contains don't do justice to the way her face becomes animated when she's excited or the infectious laughter that accompanies her million-watt smile and lights up the room around her.

The file tells me that her name is Patricia Daniels, but not that everyone calls her Trish.

It tells me she's about to turn forty years old, but not that her smooth, blemish free skin means she could pass for a woman much younger.

I know she has a daughter, Prudence, but the file doesn't reveal the depth of the love she has for her only child.

It reveals that she helped put two men behind bars, one of which is her now ex-husband but says nothing of the horror she must have felt coming home to find Diego Martinez trying to rape her teenage daughter while her husband cowered in a corner, high on heroin.

No, these are all things I've learned while we've talked and laughed over coffee, and with each day that passes I'm becoming more and more lost in her.

My gaze is drawn to her again as I watch her serve a couple at another booth. I notice how strands of her vibrant red hair have escaped from the loose bun she wears it in and how the curls frame her lovely face. I'm fascinated by the way her eyes crinkle and the little dimples that appear in her cheeks when she smiles or laughs. I want to lick those dimples and claim her lips with mine, open her mouth to my tongue so I can taste her sweetness.

I know she's been single since her divorce and on first learning this I was surprised to find myself relieved. The thought of another man in her life triggers an unwarranted jealousy. It's hard to believe a woman like her would still be single, that some man hasn't snapped her up and made her his in the years since her divorce.

Not that it matters because she's off limits. I have to keep reminding myself that I'm in no position to make a move on her, that I'm here to do a job, nothing more, nothing less. The problem is, my mission has shifted from business to personal, a dangerous change of priorities in my line of work. I can't tell her that she's part of the reason I'm here. Hopefully I won't have to if today goes as planned.

I've tried to ignore the physical pull I feel toward her but every day the tension between us seems to ratchet up another notch to the point where all I want now is to bend her back over the table, spread her legs and ease the ache she's ignited in my body between her soft thighs.

I sense her approaching my table now, so attuned am I to her presence. I look up and those vivid green eyes of hers steal my breath. I know I could lose myself in them if I look too long but I can't tear my eyes away. I notice the increased rise and fall of her breasts, her flushed cheeks, and can't help the silent satisfaction I feel at knowing she's as attracted to me as I am to her.

"More coffee, Daryl?"

The sound of my name on her lips is like an aphrodisiac and I wonder what it would be like to hear her scream it as I make her orgasm. The mental image instantly makes me hard and I'm grateful for the table which covers the blatant evidence of my arousal.

I nod in answer to her question and notice again the slight tremble of her hand as she refills my cup, telling me that she's as affected by our proximity as I am.

"Can I get you anything else?"

Now there's a question and a half. I can think of a whole multitude of things I'd like her to get me right now that aren't on the menu.

"No thanks, Trish." I hold her eyes with a smile. I'm not known for my outgoing personality but with her my smile seems to come easily.

"How's the book going?" Trish indicates the notebook on the table in front of me, referring to my cover story that I'm an author taking time out to write my latest novel.

"Well, as you can see, the words aren't exactly flowing today," I grimace, turning the notebook so she can see the blank screen.

"Hmmm. I think we need to get some inspiration for you from somewhere. It's a thriller, right?" Trish asks.

"Yeah, but nothing particularly thrilling is happening right now, apart from talking to you, of course." I grin, watching the flush that settles over her cheeks. My eyes drop to her mouth as her lips part and her tongue darts out to moisten them. Holy fuck, that's hot!

"Oh, I think you definitely need something more thrilling than that for your book," Trish jokes. "Maybe, I'm really a spy, undercover on a secret operation!" She waggles her eyebrows at me.

My laughter sounds forced as her innocent words hit too close to home. "I think I'll leave the spy stuff to Ian Fleming," I chuckle.

Trish sighs dramatically. "Oh well, it was worth a try," she grins. "Just give me a holler if you need a refill."

I watch the sexy sway of her hips under her waitressing uniform as she walks away. Does she know how perfect her ass is? How much I'd like to back her up against a wall somewhere and sink into her soft body?

Hell! I need to get a grip. I need to get my mind off her delectable curves and focus on the job at hand.

The feelings this woman engenders has me all kinds of unsettled. There's a vulnerability about Trish that brings out a part of me that wants to beat my chest, drag her to my man cave and protect her. I tell myself I'm too fucking old for this crap, that I've seen too much of the shitty side of life to believe in the concept of instant attraction or love at first sight.

In the past, my personal relationships have been few and far between and although I've wanted women, I've never *needed* them. Any intimacy with the opposite sex has been for the sole purpose of scratching an itch, nothing more. I've managed to reach the grand old age of forty-two avoiding any form of emotional commitment, no major love affairs, happy with my own company for the most part. Not to mention it would take a special kind of woman to accept the work I do, the risks involved and the kind of people I have to deal with.

I glance down at my watch. I need to get going. The diner has been the ideal place to gain Trish's trust as well as familiarize myself with the area. There's a lot riding on the success of this latest deal and I can't afford any fuck ups.

I toss a twenty on the table and stand to leave, pulling on my leather jacket. My movement catches her eye and I can feel the heat of her gaze as she looks at me, taking in everything from my booted feet and low-slung jeans to the black t-shirt beneath the jacket. It's all I can do to control the reaction of my body to her curious gaze. Whatever this thing is with her it's messing with my head and I can't afford the distraction. I need to keep my wits about me.

I quickly make my exit and head down the alley that runs alongside the diner, pulling up the collar of my jacket to keep the chill autumn wind at bay.

As I round the corner, I see the two men already waiting for me. There's an air of menace about them which others might find intimidating, but I can hold my own. I'm no lightweight at six three and two hundred pounds and I keep myself in good shape. I have to, because in my world, it could be the difference between surviving and not.

"I'm glad to see you are a man who values punctuality," the larger of the two men says with a thick Spanish accent.

"Guillermo," I nod, reaching out to shake the hand he extends toward me. Although we're similar in height, he's built like a brick shithouse, all heavy muscles and swarthy complexion. His dark hair is slicked back from his face, his expression guarded as his eyes narrow on me.

"Make sure our guest isn't carrying, Rodrigo."

I hold my jacket open as his colleague, a shorter guy with dirty blonde hair, steps forward to pat me down. I'm relying on him not doing a thorough job because I have my HK45 stashed in my boot.

"You have the money?" Guillermo asks.

I pull the wad of used bills from the inside pocket of my jacket, holding it up so he can see but not handing it to him. "I wanna see the goods," I demand.

Guillermo doesn't move for a full minute as he looks me up and down and I'm just starting to think we may have a problem when he gives a brief nod to his companion.

Rodrigo reaches into the car and pops the trunk open and I walk to the other side of the car, keeping my back to the wall behind me and my line of sight open so that no one can come up the alley without me knowing about it. Why the fuck Guillermo wanted to do the drop here, in such a confined space, I'll never know.

"It's all there," Guillermo assures me as I reach in to unzip the black holdall. As I'm lifting out one of the packets, the sound of a door opening causes all three of us to whip toward the source of the noise.

Shit! My stomach drops as Trish exits backward through the service door of the diner, struggling with a large bag of garbage. She doesn't see us straight away, absorbed as she is in her task, but as she turns, she stops short, her mouth making a silent 'O' as her eyes round in surprise.

"What the fuck?" Guillermo comes toward me, snatching the package from my hand and dropping it into the trunk before slamming it closed. But it's too late. She's already seen enough and I know that she's figured out exactly what's going on.

"I'll deal with it," I growl, putting an arm out to block Guillermo, who's about to move toward Trish.

I stride toward her, the fear I expect to see in her eyes absent. Instead, her expression is one of disgust and ...

disappointment, which makes me feel as if I've somehow failed her in some way despite her not knowing all the facts.

Before she can move, I've gathered her up against me and my lips come crashing down on hers, my tongue pushing into her mouth. I tell myself that it's got to look convincing, but the truth is, it's all too easy to get lost in her sweet mouth, the softness of her lips.

I tangle my hands through her hair and press her back into the wall behind her, my body covering hers protectively as I deepen the kiss, almost forgetting where we are.

I tear my mouth from hers, moving my lips to her ear. "You need to do exactly what I say. Go back inside, close the door and stay there." My words are a caress that only she can hear and as I draw back to look into her eyes, I see shock, and now the fear, that was missing moments ago

For a few long, seconds, she doesn't move but then she gives a jerky nod before making a hasty retreat through the door she came out of, closing it quietly behind her. I release a breath and turn back to face Guillermo.

"She your woman?" Guillermo asks in his thick accent, his eyes unusually intense. His mouth lifts in a smirk as I nod abruptly. "Shame. Would've liked a little piece of that pussy for myself, know what I mean?"

I grit my teeth at the thought of him putting his filthy hands on Trish. "Let's get this done," I growl, ignoring his words and moving back toward the car. I pull the money from my jacket and hand it to Guillermo and Rodrigo opens the trunk again.

As I bend over to retrieve the holdall I feel the cold metal of a gun muzzle pressed against the back of my head.

"Do you think I was born yesterday you stupid fuck?" Guillermo's voice is heavy with anger. "You think I don't know a cop when I see one? The fucking stink is all over you!"

I curse inwardly, knowing I've just made a mistake worthy of a rookie, that I've allowed myself to be distracted by certain redhead and put us both in danger.
My mind goes into overdrive as I consider my options. I need to stall for time but my odds are not good. Even if I can take Guillermo out, that still leaves his companion.

I have no choice but to try and bluff my way out. "Put the gun down, Guillermo. Whatever the fuck you think you know, you really don't!"

"You think you're the first *pendejo* that's tried to take me down? *No me jodas*, motherfucker! Nobody shafts me, you understand? Nobody!"

I hear the click of the gun cocking and close my eyes, knowing I'm about to become another statistic with a bullet in his brain.

TRISH

I lean back against the service door, my legs shaking not only from what I've just witnessed, but also from Daryl's unexpected kiss. Here I am going gaga over a man it seems I barely know, the same man who just backed me up against a wall and kissed me breathless. I'm not stupid, I realize it was a demonstration of ownership for the sake of appearances, but whatever his motives, the feel of his mouth on mine has left me tingling in secret places.

I can't believe that the same man I've been serving coffee to, the man I thought I'd gotten to know over the last month, is ten feet away on the other side of the door, part of some sordid drug deal.

The disappointment I feel is no surprise because I'm used to it where men are concerned. It's the feelings of hurt and the strange sense of loss that I wasn't expecting. It tells me that I'm more emotionally involved with Daryl than I realized, that I have feelings for him that have crept up on me almost unnoticed.

I lost any interest in men and the idea of intimacy well before Pete and I divorced but that all changed when Daryl walked into the diner. I was instantly attracted to him and recall with a silent groan how I'd been so flustered serving him the first time that I'd almost spilled hot coffee all over him.

His tall, lean body and ice blue eyes have awakened feelings and desires that I thought were long dead and I've found myself fantasizing about what lies beneath the leather jacket and jeans he favors.

I often feel his eyes on me when he thinks I'm not looking and his hot gaze makes me feel things that I've never felt before, even though I was married for nearly fourteen years.

I'm almost forty-years-old with a twenty-two-year old daughter and I should be beyond silly schoolgirl feelings, but there's something about Daryl that makes me feel giddy inside. The way he looks at me makes me feel young and desirable again, full of life where I've felt dead for so long. I thought my experience with Pete had killed any desire to be intimate with another man but my reaction to Daryl has turned that theory on its head.

Pete and I were typical high school sweethearts and started dating when we were fifteen. By the time I was seventeen, I was pregnant with Prue and Pete and I decided that getting married was the right thing to do.

At first things were good. Prue was born and we revelled in being new parents, enjoying her as she grew. When she was about six years old, Pete lost his job and everything changed. He changed. He became withdrawn and depressed, further exacerbated by his inability to find another job, and the distance between us grew. We were no longer intimate and most nights Pete would sleep downstairs on the sofa. He seemed to have given up on life, on us.

Pete and I grew further and further apart over the years that followed and his increasing mood swings and unpredictable temper slowly killed any feelings I had for him. The only reason I stayed was for Prue, because I mistakenly believed she deserved a family with two parents living under the same roof.

Things came to a head one day when Prue was thirteen, when a nightmare of events unfolded that I've tortured myself with endlessly ever since. I'm not sure who said that hindsight is a wonderful thing but nothing could be further from the truth. Hindsight provides nothing but pain, showing you all the things you missed, all the ways you could have done things differently.

I'm suddenly startled from my thoughts by the raised voices outside and before I can think, I've opened the door. The sight that greets me is like something out of a bad movie.

Daryl is standing by the open trunk of the car with a gun pressed to his head and despite my feelings about what's going on out here, I really don't want anyone to die, least of all him.

What happens next unfolds in a blur of activity as the sound of my unexpected reappearance unwittingly provides the perfect distraction for Daryl.

In one smooth motion, he drops to the ground, sending a kick into the kneecap of the guy holding the gun and toppling him to ground. The other guy's shriek of pain and rage echoes around the alley as Daryl reaches for something by his foot and I see a flash of metal followed by a loud pop.

I'm caught like a deer in headlights, unsure of who exactly fired the shot until the downed man's screams and curses amplify as he clutches at his leg. Daryl kicks the man's weapon, which I now see has fallen beside him on the ground, out of his reach.

"Daryl!" I scream his name, instinctively moving away from the protection of the door as I see the other man aim his weapon at him and Daryl dives behind the car as the bullet ricochets off the open lid of the trunk.

My shout has drawn the other man's attention and before I can think he's making a beeline for me. I pivot and start for the safety of the door but he's too quick and before I've taken more than a step he's grabbed a handful of my uniform, dragging me back against him and circling my throat with his other arm.

I'll be damned if I'm going down without a fight and my instincts kick in as I stomp on his foot as hard as I can. He grunts in pain, bending forward and giving me the perfect opportunity to drive my elbow up under his chin. His head whips back but he doesn't go down like I expected, like my opponents always do at my Jujitsu class. He comes at me again, only this time he's got his gun trained on me.

"Fucking bitch! You're gonna pay for th......"

The sound of another gunshot rings out and the man in front of me is spun around with the force of the bullet that hits his shoulder, before he crumbles to the ground.

Daryl keeps his gun trained on my attacker, making sure he's not getting up before swinging his aim back to the larger man on the ground, keeping his eyes locked on him as he shouts, "Are you okay, Trish?"

"Y...Yes!" My voice is a croak and I'm still breathing hard from exertion and adrenaline. Daryl pulls his phone from his jacket pocket and it takes me a few seconds to realize he's calling for backup.

Holy crap on a cracker! He's a cop!

17

"Backup's on the way. I'm sorry you got caught up in all this."
Daryl looks all steely business as he stands there, no sign of
the smiling man I've come to know over the last month.

"You're gonna fucking pay for this, Dante!" The man on the
ground spits the words at Daryl, his hands covered in blood as
he clutches at his leg.

"Name's not Dante, Guillermo. And I don't think you're in any
position to make anyone pay seeing as you're the one on the
ground with a bullet hole in your leg."

"How do you think I knew you were a cop, you stupid
asshole?" Guillermo taunts. "Watch your back, Dante, or
whatever the fuck your name is. It's difficult to know who you
can trust in your line of work."

The sound of approaching sirens halts any further discussion
as two police cars come screaming up the alley, four armed
officers immediately out of their vehicles with their guns
trained on not only the two downed men, but Daryl and myself.

Daryl holds his gun up, index finger through the trigger and
muzzle facing down as stoops to place the weapon on the
ground, dropping to his knees and placing his hands behind
his head.

Backup has arrived.

The next hour passes in a daze as Daryl's identity is verified
and EMT's arrive to treat the injured men. Daryl leads me
back inside the diner which is now empty, cleared of
customers for their own safety.

Barbara, my friend and the owner of the diner, is the only one that remains, having refused to leave until she knew I was safe, even when they threatened to arrest her. The woman, although a force to be reckoned with, has a heart as big as the open sky and put a roof over mine and Prue's heads until we got back on our feet after we left our old life behind.

She puts a cup of strong coffee in front of me, patting my arm. "Here you go, honey. This will help. I'm so glad you're okay. I can't believe what just happened out there!"

"Thanks, Barb." I squeeze her hand and give her a feeble smile before taking a sip of the strong brew. I sigh as it leaves a hot, soothing trail down my throat, warming the ball of ice that seems to have settled in my stomach.

Daryl slides into the booth next to me, along with a uniformed officer. "You feel up to giving a statement?" His warm hand clasps mine where it rests on the table, and despite everything that's happened, his touch is soothing.

I nod and give as much information to the officer as I can, all the while hyper aware of the warmth of Daryl's body next to me, his muscular thigh pressing against mine.

"Come on. I'll take you home," Daryl says, once the officer is happy he has everything he needs and has left.

"No, no. It's fine. I can walk. It's not far," I protest.

"You're not walking anywhere," Daryl insists. "You've had a shock and I'm not leaving you alone."

His words warm me and if I'm honest, I'm not doing too well with this whole situation. Now that the adrenaline has worn off, old fears and memories are coming back to haunt me, making me feel more than a little shaky.

I nod in agreement and look up to see Barb bustling up to the table with my purse and coat.

"Get yourself home, honey, and I don't want to see you here for the next few days. I've already called Helena and she'll cover for you. And don't worry about your wages, I'll make sure they're covered too," Barb adds, anticipating all my protests.

I'm touched by her thoughtfulness and hug her warmly as Daryl and I stand to leave. Barb knows I struggle to make my rent some months, especially while I'm also paying my fees for my counselling degree.

Daryl leads me outside to his car, a Dodge, and walks around to open my door. I climb into the passenger seat and reach for my seatbelt but his hands are there first, his body leaning over me, his fingers brushing my thigh as he secures it.

He pauses as he hears my intake of breath at the contact, his face mere inches from mine, his eyes lingering on my mouth and for a second I think he's going to close the small gap between us and kiss me. And, oh Lordy, do I want his mouth on mine again! The moment passes and he straightens, walking to the driver's side, climbing in and starting the engine.

As he drives, the tension stretches between us until it feels like a thread about to snap.

"What you did back there, how you handled that guy, was amazing," Daryl says, finally breaking the loaded silence.

I'm still reeling from the whole experience and his words remind me that, despite my efforts, I'd probably be dead if it weren't for him. "I've been taking self-defence classes for years. I thought it was only fair as I made Prue, my daughter, take them after…uh…when she was younger."

If Daryl notices my little slip, he doesn't let on. "You saved my life. If you hadn't reappeared when you did..."

"I'm pretty sure you've got that backward. If I hadn't blundered out there in the first place, I'm sure it would've all gone down differently." I'm aware that my unexpected presence the first time around most likely spooked the other men.

"Not your fault." Daryl's voice is firm. "I got sloppy. I seem to be doing that a lot just recently." His eyes slide across to me and I feel my cheeks heat at his insinuation that I'm the reason for the sloppiness. "Not noticing there was a service door was a rookie mistake."

"It is hard to see with all the graffiti," I say, trying to make him feel better. "I'm just glad you're okay. When I saw that man with the gun to your head, I thought..." I let my words trail off.

"Yeah. Me too." Daryl gives me a wry smile, before tearing his eyes away and making the turn into the quiet cul-de-sac where my apartment is located.

"How do you know where I live?" I ask, suddenly remembering that I never gave him my address.

"There are a lot of things I know about you, Trish, including where you live," Daryl says, giving me what looks like a remorseful look. "I know that your ex-husband is in jail and why he's there. If you're up to it, I'd like to come in and discuss just how I know those things."

My heart skips at his words. "You haven't been coming to the diner purely for the great coffee, have you?"

Daryl shakes his head, pinning me with his gaze. "No. Amongst other reasons, I was there for you."

DARYL

I watch the expressions of shock and disbelief chase across Trish's face as she tries to make sense of my words, the internal battle going on as she debates whether she wants to know more.

Curiosity wins out and she nods. "You'd better come in."

Trish unlocks the door to her apartment and I glance around as I follow her through the entrance hall and into the living area. It's small but tastefully decorated, the living and dining area open plan with what looks to be a bedroom leading off it, and a small but fully fitted kitchen.

"It's not much, but it's home," Trish says, as she kicks off her sneakers and walks to the kitchen, taking two cups down from one of the cupboards.

"It's great," I assure her, knowing how hard she must have worked to keep a roof over both her and her daughter's heads, particularly before Prue went off to college. "You've made it feel homely."

There are several framed photographs on a side table and I pick one up, knowing instantly that the young, smiling girl in the picture is Trish's daughter. Same vibrant red hair, same emerald green eyes but Prue has a smattering of freckles across her nose where Trish's complexion is clear.

Trish walks into the room and sees me holding the photograph. "My daughter, Prue, when she was about twelve-years-old."

I can hear the love and pride in Trish's voice and something squeezes at my heart, a deep-seated need in me wanting to hear her say my name with the same level of emotion. Shit, I'm getting soft in my old age. She's making me want things that have never even been on my radar before.

"She looks a lot like you," I say, placing the photograph down carefully and turning to take the mug of coffee from Trish who has come to stand behind me. Our fingers brush and I can feel the tremble of her hand at the contact. It's all I can do not to drop the damn coffee on the floor and pull her into my arms again, kiss her like I did earlier in the alley, only this time without the audience and imminent threat of death.

Trish moves to the sofa and takes a seat, curling her feet up underneath her and indicating for me to take the chair opposite. "So, you mentioned my ex-husband?"

I nod, leaning forward to place my cup on the coffee table in front of me, deciding how best to explain everything to her. "I've been undercover for the last year, working on a drugs case. We know there's a big player at its center but we don't know who. Those guys today were just a means to an end, a

23

way for me to get to whoever the guy is at the top and try to crack the case wide open."

I can see Trish's eyes widening as she listens and wonder if this will all be too much for her after the ordeal of today. "So, what has all this got to do with me? With my ex-husband?"

I notice with admiration that her voice is steady, reflecting none of the inner turmoil I know she must be feeling. She's tougher than she looks and I feel an unexpected pang of pride at how well she's holding up.

"The big guy today, the one I shot in the leg, is called Guillermo Martinez." Trish blanches as she recognises the man's last name. "He has a brother called Diego, whom I know you've been unfortunate enough to cross paths with."

I pause, looking directly into Trish's eyes. "I know all about what happened, Trish. About Peter's drug dealings and his own habit. How he stood back and allowed another man to almost rape his thirteen-year-old daughter. How the only reason Diego Martinez didn't succeed was because you came home early."

"You have my file," Trish whispers, dropping her head into her heads when she sees my nod. "Oh, God! I can't go through all this again!"

Instinctively, I move next to her on the sofa, taking her cold hands in mine. "Guillermo and Diego Martinez work for the man we're trying to identify. All we know is that he goes by the name of Salvadore. We know that's not his real name but we have very little to go on as he never gets his hands dirty with what he considers to be the mundane aspects of the business. Very few people outside his immediate circle know who he is, what he looks like. But we have reason to believe that you might."

Trish lifts shocked eyes to mine, her green eyes even more startling against the pallor of her skin. "What do you mean?"

"We think that you've seen him, that he came to your house and threatened Peter when he found out that he was skimming off the top, stealing gear for his own personal use."

Trish frowns. "But why would he waste time on someone like Pete? Why not send one of his lackeys to do the dirty work?"

"He did. When Pete didn't heed the warning, he sent Diego Martinez but his instructions were not to harm Peter. Prue was the target to make sure Peter got the message loud and clear, that he didn't step out of line again. What we don't know is why Peter was untouchable. We're guessing that he had something on Salvadore, something that prevented Salvadore from killing him because he's killed others for less. Maybe not by his own hand, but certainly on his orders."

Trish lets out a shaky breath. "I can't believe he sent a man to rape a thirteen-year-old girl! This is so much bigger than I ever imagined! Why do you think I can identify this man? The only person I ever saw was Diego Martinez the day he attacked Prue."

"Because I paid Pete a visit in jail and he told me that you were there the night Salvadore came to the house," I explain. "He wouldn't give me any other information because he didn't want to put you or Prue in harm's way again."

Trish pauses, her brow furrowed in concentration, as if trying to recall some long-forgotten memory. "A man did come to the house, a few months before Martinez attacked Prue. It was late at night and I'd already gone to bed when I heard voices downstairs. I got up and went to the top of the stairs to listen and Pete was in the kitchen, talking to another man. I couldn't make out what was being said and a minute later he left. I only saw him from the back and he was wearing one of those long overcoats, so I couldn't really see much of his body, other than he was tall with broad shoulders and blonde hair."

Trish lifts her eyes to mine. "I never gave it another thought with everything that happened after that and when I asked Pete about it he said it was just someone he knew who could repair the faulty laptop I'd been nagging him about. That's all I can remember. I'm sorry."

I sigh, knowing it's not enough, but not wanting Trish to feel bad. "What you've told me has been helpful, Trish. Do you think you'd be able to recognise him if you saw him again?" I try not to look as if I'm hanging on her answer.

Trish shrugs one shoulder. "I don't know. Like I said, I didn't see his face clearly."

"Any information you can give us to identify him will help, Trish, maybe give us enough evidence to stop him from fucking up any more lives." Part of me hates having to pressure her like this.

She lifts watery green eyes to mine. "What would it involve?"

"In the first instance, I'd take you down to the station and get you to look through some mug shots, see if anyone looks familiar."

"And if I don't recognise anyone?"

I sigh. "Let's cross that bridge when we get to it, okay?"

Trish falls silent, weighing up all that I've told her. "This is your only option now, isn't it? Your cover was blown today, thanks to me."

I can feel the tremble of her body against me, firing off all kinds of primal instincts that I'm trying not to act on. "No.

Thanks to me, Trish. I take full responsibility for putting you in that position, putting you in danger."

Trish looks at me directly, her gaze open, revealing the core of strength that runs through her. "I'll do it. On one condition. Under no circumstances is Prue to be involved. Not in any way, shape or form."

"You have my word, Trish. The last thing I want to do is put either of you in danger, especially after what happened today," I promise. "When you came through that door I was more scared about you getting hurt than I was about the deal being fucked up. That's why I kissed you. I knew if Guillermo thought you were my woman, I could keep you safe, get you out of there."

"I knew that was why," Trish says, smiling wryly. "I'm not stupid. I know you wouldn't have kissed me otherwise. I realize that all of this," she moves her hand back and forth between us, "was all part of the act."

"Is that what you really think, Trish? That it was all part of my cover?" I move away from her slightly so I can see her face. I sigh resignedly at her look, knowing that she truly believes everything was an act on my part and the next words spill from my mouth before I can think. "I was never supposed to be dealing with your case, Trish. My responsibility was Guillermo. Another operative was assigned to you but as soon as I saw your file, I knew it had to be me. So, I pulled a few strings to make it happen."

"From seeing my file? Why?" Trish asks, genuinely curious.

"There were a couple of pictures of you in the file that were taken during the trial. They weren't the best quality, but there was something about you, about your expression in one of them, that I couldn't get out of my head. You looked so lost, so lonely. Yet, there was something in your eyes, a strength that

27

said you weren't going to give up or give in to the hand you'd been dealt."

I see the tears on Trish's cheeks and curse myself. "Shit! I'm sorry! I didn't mean to upset you." I cup her face, brushing away her tears with my thumbs. "I've fought this attraction I feel for you, Trish, because I had a job to do and told myself I couldn't afford the distraction but the truth is I haven't stopped thinking about you since the day I walked into the diner. That was the day the woman in those pictures became a reality and I knew I was lost."

I lean closer, my mouth hovering over hers. "This isn't some elaborate act, Trish. Every day since I met you I've imagined what it would be like to kiss you. Touch you." There's no going back now - I've just laid it all out there against my better judgment not to get involved but it's already too late for that. It's been too late for a while now.

Trish's eyes widen at my confession. "You have?"

"I have," I whisper, my breath fanning over her lips. "All I can think about is whether you taste as good as I think you do."

Trish's breath catches at my words and it's all I need to close the inch that separates us and claim her mouth, teasing her lips open to the invasion of my tongue. The taste of her lights a fire in my blood and suddenly I can't get enough, the kiss becoming needy and rough as she matches my passion, pushing her hands through my hair as she holds me to her. I gather her against me, wanting her closer, needing more of her soft body against my hardness, my desire for her overriding rational thought as my hands reach for the buttons of her uniform.

Trish arches her back, her body inviting me to slip buttons from button holes and my heart almost explodes in my chest at her silent invitation. My mouth crashes against hers as I devour her and she matches me, kiss for kiss, our tongues tangling hungrily. The last four weeks of heated glances and soft touches, along with the heightened emotions of our earlier scrape with death have led us to this moment, our need for each other exploding in a rage of need and desire.

I break the kiss and pull her to her feet, smoothing the now unbuttoned uniform from her shoulders and watching as it slides down her curves, my breath catching as she stands before me in her black bra and panties. I still the hands that she moves to instinctively cover herself, twining her fingers through mine.

"Don't hide yourself from me, Trish." I move her hands down to the front of my jeans, pressing them against my hard shaft with a groan as I show her just how much I want her. "That's what you do to me. I'm just as vulnerable as you are, just as much at the mercy of whatever this is between us."

Trish takes a deep breath and steps into my body, pulling my head down to claim my mouth in a blistering kiss. I need her closer and gather her against my body as I slide my hands around her waist and down the back of her panties, grasping her rounded ass and pulling her into my hips, pressing my swollen shaft against the heat of her pussy.

Trish tears her mouth away and threads her fingers through mine, leading me through to the bedroom and toward the bed. She slides my jacket from my shoulders and reaches for the hem of my t-shirt, tugging it up so that I lift my arms as she stands on her tiptoes to slide it over my head. Her soft hands land on my chest, her fingers a whisper against my skin as she traces my muscles, my abs clenching as her hands skim over them to unbutton my jeans, sliding them down my hips.

I kick them off but there's still too much clothing between us and as if reading my thoughts, Trish hooks her thumbs into the waistband of my boxers, bending to slide them down my hips and thighs and releasing my engorged shaft.

She kneels before me and before I can think, she takes me in her warm mouth and I can barely breathe for the spasm of pleasure that shoots from my balls to my swollen cock as her tongue sweeps around me, her mouth working all kinds of magic.

"Jesus, Trish! That feels fucking amazing!" I gasp. "If you keep that up, I'm not gonna last long."

Trish releases my swollen shaft from her mouth and looks up, her eyes glazed with desire. "Then don't."

Her mouth envelops my cock again, driving me insane as she swallows the full impressive length of me, sucking and licking until I can't help the small thrusts of my hips against her. I feel my orgasm fast approaching and wonder if I'm going to survive it.

"Fuck, Trish!" I can feel my neck muscles cording as I throw my head back, tangling my hands in her hair and holding her to me as I gasp out my orgasm, unloading my cum into her mouth in short spurts. It takes everything I have to remain upright as every muscle in my body quivers at the force of my release, the sight of her swallowing my seed only heightening my pleasure.

My breathing begins to return to normal as Trish looks up at me. "Was it okay? I've never done this before. Pete didn't like it if I took control."

I can't believe what she's telling me and I pull her up so that she's within reach of my mouth, kissing her softly and running my tongue across her lips, tasting my cum on her which unbelievably makes me hard all over again. "My, God Trish. It was perfect! You were perfect. You just about blew my fucking head off!"

Trish smiles against my mouth, the flush of embarrassment and pleasure covering her cheeks tugging at my heart.

"And now I get to return the favor." I reach behind her, releasing the catch of her bra and sliding the straps down her shoulders, watching as her magnificent tits spill forth, her nipples hard and begging for my mouth.

I cup them in my hands, bending to place my mouth against her warm skin and pulling one nipple into my mouth, suckling and stroking it with my tongue while I pinch the other nipple between my thumb and forefinger. Her moan causes the pulse between my legs to throb with a new need, something that should be impossible after the release she just gave me.

I tug her toward the bathroom, reaching into the shower cubicle to turn on the jets before divesting her of the last of her clothing by sliding her panties down her silky legs.

We step under the warm spray and I squeeze some soap into my hand, lathering it between my palms. I turn Trish so that her back is to me and sweep my hands around her shoulders, kneading her tight muscles until she sighs and leans back against me.

"That feels amazing." Her voice is husky with pleasure as I move my hands down her arms, spreading the suds and trying to ease away the stresses of the day. I scoop my hands around to her stomach, sweeping them over her lush curves and up to cup her perfect tits, the soap making my fingers slick as I tease her nipples, palming the hard nubs and making her moan. The sound causes my cock to swell against her back and I move my hips so that my rigid shaft slides between the cleft of her ass cheeks with a friction that almost has me shooting my load again.

I slide my hands down her stomach and into the tangle of hair between her thighs, opening her pussy lips to my seeking fingers as I slip one finger along her slit, moving back and forth along the hard nub of her clit.

31

Trish moans and arches against my hand and I feel the tremble of her legs as she grinds herself against me. I increase the pressure of my finger, sliding a second finger inside her tight hole, pumping it in and out until she's gasping my name and I feel the contractions as she quickly goes over the edge.

"My God, Daryl!" She cries out as her orgasm hits her and I feel the slickness of her love juices on my fingers as her body spasms against me, her back arching as she seeks to hold on to the intense pleasure surging through her body. Her legs give way and I pull her to me, turning her so I can take her weight and hold her against me as she comes down from her high.

"Oh, my goodness." She's still breathing heavily as she looks up and our eyes lock. Something passes between us, something unspoken but powerful as we stand there, the water rushing over our bodies as we cling together.

I reach over and turn off the shower and as we step out Trish grabs us both a towel, looping hers around my neck and using it to pull me down for her kiss, our mouths heated, our desire for each other not yet sated.

She tears her mouth away. "What are we doing here, Daryl?" she asks, her green eyes holding mine.

"I think that's fairly obvious." My voice is gruff with passion as I pull her hair to one side, finding the sensitive spot where her neck meets her shoulder and nipping it lightly with my teeth. I feel her shudder as her neck arches, allowing me greater access to her soft skin.

"I mean, what is this? Is this just physical attraction? Is it something...more?"

I lean in to kiss her softly, gently. "I want you, Trish. I've never been in love, never been close, so I don't know what it feels like. I guess I've always thought I would just know. But if it's caring about another person's safety more than your own, thinking about them every hour of the day, wanting to protect them, hold them, make love to them, then I'm already in deep. Because that's how I feel about you."

Trish pulls my head down again, kissing me deeply. "Show me," she breathes against my mouth.

With a groan, I back her up toward the bedroom, my mouth never leaving hers as we topple onto the bed in tangle of limbs. I'm careful not to crush her as I settle on top of her, but she seems to revel in the weight of my body pressing her into the mattress, her hips moving rhythmically below me as she seeks a deeper contact.

"Are you sure about this?" I growl against her mouth.

"Too late now," she smiles at me, running her hands over my shoulders and down my back to grasp my butt as she opens her legs and wraps them around my hips, pulling me toward her so that my cock is positioned against her slick opening. "Just take it easy though. I haven't done this for a long time."

"How long?" I ask, feathering kisses along the swell of her tits.

"Sixteen years, give or take."

"Sixteen years? But..." I look at her in shock, unable to grasp the concept that Trish hasn't been with a man for that length of time.

"Pete and I stopped being intimate after he lost his job. He lost all interest in life. In me," she murmurs.

I close my eyes, imagining how that must have felt. This woman deserves to be worshipped, body and mind, made to feel as special as she is.

"Then he was a fucking fool!" I say, rolling onto my back in one smooth motion and bringing Trish with me so that she's straddling my hips. "You're in control of this," I say, reaching up to her breasts and running my fingers over the nubs of her nipples, watching as her eyes close and she arches her back to deepen the contact.

I grit my teeth and force myself to lie still as Trish positions herself over me, taking the end of my cock into her slowly as eases down a little and then up again, her tight channel absorbing a little more of my length each time as her body to adjusts to this kind of intimacy again.

Finally, she lets out a sigh and begins to move against me, finding the right position, her internal muscles squeezing the length of my cock with each pass as she rides me.

When I can't stand it any longer, I thrust up into her waiting body as she sinks down on me, filling her completely, the sensation of our bodies coming together making us both cry out.

"Are you okay?" I manage to gasp, not wanting to hurt her, even now.

"More than okay," she moans, as my hands grip her hips, holding her against me with each thrust of my body. "I've been married, given birth to a child, but you're bordering on virgin territory."

Her words excite me, knowing that I am making her feel something she's never felt before. I quicken my pace, my cock slamming up into her and I can already feel the pleasure building in my balls. I know I'm not going to last much longer but sense that Trish needs more time to reach her orgasm.

34

I force myself to stop, still buried deep within her as I reach down and open her slick folds to my fingers, rubbing her clit until she's bucking and gasping against me. I slowly increase the rhythm of my hips again, maintaining the contact of my fingers on her wet pussy as I press her nub like a button with each thrust of my hips.

Her thighs tighten around my hips and I know she's about to cum, watching as she throws her head back and screams my name. The sight is so fucking sexy that I feel my own orgasm slam into me, her tight channel milking every last drop of cum from my cock as I pour my hot seed into her in a climax unlike anything I've ever felt.

Trish collapses against my chest, breathing hard as we both recover from the intensity of our lovemaking.

I'm still catching my breath as she climbs off me and heads to the bathroom to clean up. She's back quickly and I pull her to me, her body fitting perfectly against mine as my hands roam her curves, unable to stop touching her soft skin.

"That was amazing." She looks up at me and grins, her whole face aglow with the aftermath of our loving. "It was never like that with Pete, not even when we were first together. I'm beginning to realise what I've missed out on all these years. I think you may have unleashed my inner sex addict!"

I growl and pull her even closer, nuzzling my mouth against her neck. "As long as it's only with me. No one else gets to see your inner sex addict but me." I bite her earlobe gently, feeling very possessive over this woman in my arms.

"You don't have any worries there. I thought I'd forgotten how. You were definitely worth the wait!"

"Careful. I won't be able to fit my head back out the door!" I chuckle, loving this feeling of being with her as much as the sex that came before it. Okay, maybe not quite as much, but close.

"What about you?" Trish asks, her fingers tracing idle circles on my chest. "We've talked over the last few weeks but I obviously don't really know anything about you. I had no idea you were a cop. Which, I guess, was the whole point."

"For what it's worth, I'm sorry." I say. "When I walked into the diner that first day, I had no idea that meeting you was going to change everything. By the time I realized how involved I was I couldn't risk blowing my cover without putting us both in danger, even though that's exactly what happened anyway," I finish wryly.

"I'm sorry but I can't help but question the time we spent together when all along you were gathering information," Trish sighs, her voice full of uncertainty.

"That's how it started, honey, but that's not how it ended," I say, placing my fingers under her chin and tipping her head back so that she can see the sincerity in my eyes. "It got so I couldn't wait to see you every day, talk to you, learn more about you. Not because of the job but because I wanted to get to know you, the real you."

I smooth her hair back from her face. "You and I were always going to meet, Trish. Whether it was now, next month, or in a year's time. Under different circumstances, things would have developed naturally between us. I would have asked you out on a date, wined and dined you just like you deserve, and we would have ended up exactly where we are right now because, God knows, what I feel for you was meant to be."

Trish releases a shaky breath at my words. "It was the same for me, from the minute you walked into the diner. Then I saw you in the alley and everything came crashing down around me. It was like history repeating itself," she grimaces. "When you kissed me, I realized you were doing it to protect me and

36

that things weren't quite what they seemed. Seeing that man holding a gun to your head terrified me because I suddenly knew that if you died my world would be colder without you in it."

"Thanks to you, that didn't happen," I say, leaning in to kiss her softly, my hands falling to her hips and pulling her against me.

"Thank God!" Trish says passionately. "It could have ended so differently, for both of us."

"But it didn't, honey." I roll over, pinning her to the mattress below me, my body making unbelievable demands where this woman is concerned.

Her eyes widen as she feels my body swell against hers. "Again?"

"Again," I growl. It's going to be a long time, if ever, before I've had my fill of this woman.

TRISH

The room is in darkness when I wake. Instinctively, I reach for Daryl and my hands find empty space, the only proof he was here the dent in the pillow and the unfamiliar soreness of my body.

I glance at the bedside clock. Eight in the evening - we've spent all afternoon in bed. I must have fallen asleep after our last lovemaking session. I never knew I could have such an endless passion for one man, for the things he made me feel.

I've thrown myself head first into this whole thing, whatever it is, and a niggle of doubt creeps into my mind, whispering that Daryl is using me to get the information he needs. I push it down, not prepared to consider that what we just shared was premeditated, that he would be cruel enough to lure me into bed for the sake of the case when I've already agreed to help.

Can I finally allow myself to be happy? To move on with my life? Could Daryl be the one to help me do that? Despite the short time we've known each other, I feel as if my soul has been waiting for him, recognized its true mate the second he walked into the diner.

I've been living in a vacuum for years, not moving backward but not moving forward either. Pete's choices have impacted both Prue and myself far more than we ever imagined. The repercussions of his dealings, the people he got involved with, have continued to bleed into our lives even though I haven't seen my ex-husband since he was imprisoned.

As a mother, the hardest thing for me to bear is knowing that my decision to stay damaged not only me, but Prue as well. A mother should protect her young, and I failed miserably by not seeing what was going on underneath my nose, not recognising the signs that my husband was an addict and a dealer, and those shortcomings have tormented me for years.

I still torture myself with the 'what ifs' of the day that Prue was attacked. What if I hadn't come home early? What if we hadn't been able to get away from Martinez? What if I'd left Pete when I realized our relationship was dead instead of hanging on to empty marriage vows and even emptier promises from him that things would get better. I should have known that they never would.

Not that Prue has ever blamed or resented me in any way - I've done that all by myself. She's the very best thing that came out of my relationship with Pete and I miss her terribly now she's living almost three hundred miles away in Bakersfield. She deserves some happiness in her life, someone who'll help her heal her own wounds and move on from the past.

As for me, I had no interest in any form of relationship after Pete until I clapped eyes on Daryl. There's always been a part of me that feels I don't deserve to be happy after everything that's happened, but for the first time in a long time, I have hope. Hope that maybe, just maybe, I can move on with my life.

The rumbling of my stomach interrupts my train of thought, reminding me that I haven't eaten for several hours.

I climb out of bed and grab my robe, heading through the living room to the kitchen. I notice a yellow note stuck to the kitchen cabinet, my mouth curving into a smile as I read the masculine scrawl.

Had some business to take care of. This afternoon was amazing. Call you later. D

I wonder if the business involves what happened earlier today and the ongoing investigation into Salvadore. I'm sure that Daryl has things he needs to do now that his cover has been blown.

I make myself a sandwich and eat it in front of the TV while half-heartedly watching the local news, wondering if there's anything about the events of today. There isn't and I suspect that the whole thing has been kept quiet.

Once I've finished eating, I decide to call Prue, needing to hear her voice after all that's happened today.

"Hey, Mom." She answers my call on the second ring.

Hearing Prue's voice always calms me in a way nothing else can. "Hey, sweet girl. How are you? How's work?"

"Good, but tiring. This earning your own living thing is hard work!"

I chuckle. "You don't need to tell me that, honey. It's a good feeling though, standing on your own two feet. Seriously, are

40

you managing okay? I know what it's like trying to make rent and pay all the bills."

"No one knows that better than you, Mom," Prue sighs down the phone. "But, I'm fine. I have new neighbors who've just moved in next door, an elderly couple who seem really sweet. Mr. Grimes is recovering from a hip operation, so we got talking about his recovery. You know I'm a sucker for anything health related," Prue laughs.

"You have a passion for what you do, Prue, and that will take you a long way." I feel a surge of pride for all that my daughter has achieved despite such a rocky start in life. Then I remember the reason for that rocky start and the memories ignite the touch-paper that is my guilt.

"Talking of having a passion, how's the counselling going?" Prue asks.

"Really good. Only another couple of months and I'll be done." I enrolled in an online Master of Arts in Counselling degree three years ago which allows me to build my counselling skills without relocating.

"I'm really proud of you, Mom. For turning your life around, creating something good for yourself out of a bad situation."

I swallow the lump in my throat at Prue's words. "Thank you, honey. Not that I deserve your lovely words. None of us would've been in the situation we were if I'd left your father sooner."

Prue's frustrated sigh reaches me clearly down the phone line. "Mom, seriously! How many times are we going to have this conversation? It wasn't your fault! Dad is responsible for his own crappy choices and we're living with the consequences. He's the one who should be blaming himself, not you."

"I'm not sure I'll ever stop blaming myself, Prue. But I am trying to let the past go." I debate whether to tell Prue my news and decide that I want her to know. Maybe if she sees me moving forward with my life it will encourage her to do the same. "I've, uh, I've even met someone. His name's Daryl."

"What? You waited this far into the conversation to tell me?" Prue shrieks. "That's great news, Mom! Now, I need to know everything..."

An hour later I say goodbye to Prue, having survived the inquisition of questions. I told her how Daryl and I met and that he's a cop but left out what happened in the alley. The least she knows, the better, for her own protection. I may have failed in protecting her in the past but I'll be damned if I'm going to fail her again. No, if I'm going to help Daryl with this case then it's better if Prue knows nothing about it and I'm trusting Daryl on his word that she won't be involved.

I stifle a yawn as tiredness overtakes me again, the events of the day having taken their toll. I climb back into bed, pulling the pillow where Daryl lay earlier to my nose and inhaling the masculine scent that has become so familiar to me in such a short space of time.

As if my thoughts have summoned him, my phone vibrates on the bedside cabinet and his name pops up on the caller ID. I smile as I realize he's somehow managed to program his number into my phone.

"Hello."

"Hey, you." The sound of Daryl's deep timbre makes my insides melt.

"I see you managed to break and enter my phone," I accuse, tongue in cheek.

"One of the tricks of the trade," he chuckles. "You doing okay, honey?"

"I'm doing good. Where are you?" I ask.

"At work. Sorry I had to leave but I had some paperwork to tie up so that I can be integrated back into plainclothes now that I'm officially no longer undercover."

"It's okay. I understand. I missed you when I woke up though, the bed already feels empty without you," I murmur.

"This afternoon was amazing, Trish. *You* are amazing." His voice drops to a growl. "If I was there with you now, I'd be burying myself inside you again, making you scream my name as you cum, just like you did earlier."

His words reignite the throb between my thighs and I smother a moan. "If you were here I'd like that, feeling you deep inside me," I whisper.

"I'd go so deep, honey. Is that sweet pussy of yours wet for me? Put your hands there and tell me how much you wish I was there with you now, putting my mouth on you."

"Daryl!" I moan, his words turning me on. I slip my hand down and open my slick folds, finding my clit with my finger. "I'm so wet for you, Daryl. I wish you were here!"

"I know, honey. Imagine I'm there, that it's my hands on you, my fingers rubbing that juicy clit of yours until you cum."

I increase the rhythm and friction of my fingers, closing my eyes and imagining Daryl with me, his mouth on my nipples as

43

he licks them to hard peaks, his thick shaft pumping in and out of my body.

"Dear God!" I bite my lip as my climax hits me and it's even more intense knowing that Daryl can hear me as I gasp my release down the phone. I seem to have a never-ending supply of orgasms where this man is concerned.

"Jesus, Trish! Do you know how sexy that was? Hearing you get off like that? I'm so fucking hard for you right now!"

I catch my breath. "Wow! Well, that was a first. I can safely say I've never done anything like that before." I flush at my complete abandonment of the last few minutes, my mind still trying to catch up with how sensitive my body is where he's concerned.

"Me neither, if I'm honest," Daryl admits. "Just seemed like the natural thing to do with you. You'll sleep well now. I'll see you tomorrow, honey."

"Tomorrow?"

"Yeah, I'll pick you up about three and bring you down to the station to look at those mug shots."

I hadn't realized he would want to do it so soon, but I guess it's better to get it over and done with. "Okay. I'll see you at three. Sleep well."

"No chance of that now. Not after hearing you moan down the phone like that," Daryl groans.

"I'll just say sweet dreams until tomorrow, then," I laugh.

"Night, Trish."

"Night, Daryl."

I end the call and toss the phone on the bedside cabinet, snuggling down in bed and clutching Daryl's pillow to me as I succumb to sleep.

DARYL

I'm pretty sure my cock is never going to go down after that phone call, despite the afternoon Trish and I spent in bed together. It's just as well I'm on my own in the office, or my colleagues may have been privy to a whole new side of me that they've never seen before. But, goddamn, if that wasn't one of the hottest things I've ever heard, the sound of Trish bringing herself to orgasm on the other end of the line.

I push down the pang of guilt at how I allowed things to happen between us this afternoon. I could be jeopardising the case by getting involved with Trish but I just can't seem to stay away from her. My need for her has only gotten worse now I've tasted her sweetness, been buried inside her soft body. I'd still be there now if I had my way, but I needed to get back here to make a start on the mountain of paperwork required to reintegrate me back into normal police duties.

Resettling back into the normal police role means shedding the habits that have become a way of life and being able to accept the discipline of superiors again. Cops that are UC for a long period of time, sometimes many years, often find it much harder, having abandoned the normal rules for so long.

I've heard stories of UC cops who've become addicts, or worse, have switched sides, sympathising with the very criminals they were sent to take down. I've only been undercover for a year which will make the whole transition easier for me.

I need to speak with my handler and let him know what the situation is in case he hasn't already been briefed. All evidence of John Dante, my UC identity, needs to be destroyed and I'll be glad to have my police badge and Glock back. I'm also looking forward to returning to my own apartment as the UC residence never really felt like home.

Using the cell phone for the last time before it's submitted for evidence, I dial Lev's number.

"It's Dante." I automatically use my UC identity, as is procedure but then give him my code to stand down on the operation.

"What the fuck happened?" Lev's voice booms at me down the line.

"That's what I'd like to know," I reply. "Guillermo got twitchy and I ended up with a gun to my head. Fortunately, I caught a break in the form of a distraction and was able to take both him and Rodrigo down."

"Shit! What was the distraction?" Lev asks curiously. Typical of him to ignore the whole 'me almost dying' part.

Up to this point, Trish's identity hasn't been exposed to anyone, not even Lev, for her own protection. "The redhead that works in the diner. She interrupted us taking out the garbage and I had to do some…damage limitation."

"Is she still alive?"

"Yeah, she's safe. I managed to convince Guillermo that she was my woman, that I had it under control - or so I thought." I grimace, remembering how close a call it had been.

"Why the fuck was the drop in the back alley in the first place?" Lev sounds pissed.

"Not my call," I defend myself. "I didn't get to choose where the drop went down. That was down to Guillermo. The part that *is* down to me is not checking that there were rear access points - a mistake not even a cop who's wet behind the ears would make and one I'll probably never forgive myself for."

"Happens to the best of us under pressure," Lev states. "So, the redhead, what's her name?"

"Trish Daniels." Saying her name makes me want to rush over to her apartment and wrap her in my arms again.

"Is she the one who might be able to identify Salvadore?" Lev's asks, and I can hear the urgency in his voice. He's just as invested in bringing him down as I am.

"I was hoping she might, but it's looking doubtful. She remembers seeing him a few months before she left her ex-husband, but it was late at night and she only saw him from the back. I'm bringing her in tomorrow to look at some mug shots, but I'm not holding out much hope."

I can hear Lev's sigh down the phoneline. "Well, shit! Let's hope our redhead can surprise us and come up with the goods."

"Yeah. Let's hope, Lev."

After my phone call with Lev, I call it a night, pick up a pizza and head back to my old apartment.

There's a comforting familiarity about the place as I walk in, despite the slightly unlived-in smell. Everything is exactly as I left it and the utilities and rent have all been paid in my absence so I don't have to worry about getting anything reconnected.

After I've demolished the pizza I make up the king-size bed in my bedroom before heading for the shower. That phone call with Trish has been burning a hole in my brain and I'm in need of some relief.

Climbing under the spray, I take myself in hand, palming my rigid cock as I remember Trish's mouth on me earlier. Just the thought of her tongue swirling around the sensitive end of my shaft has me increasing my tempo, pounding my hand up and down my length until, with a grunt of satisfaction, I shoot my load, my cum merging with the spray from the shower.

I dry myself off and collapse into bed, wishing that Trish's warm body was next to me, wrapping herself around me like she had earlier when she fell asleep, exhausted from the amazing sex we'd shared.

I still can't believe that I was her first man for so many years, only the second man she's ever been with.

I plan to be the last.

Trish answers the door to her apartment at my knock the following afternoon. Before she can speak, I've backed her up, closing the door behind me and pulled her into my arms, my mouth descending on hers.

Trish returns my kiss with interest as I push her up against the wall, pressing my hardness against her soft curves, her body built to fit mine perfectly.

I grab her hips, pulling her against the bulge of my needy cock and she moans, threading her fingers through my hair as she holds me to her, pushing her tongue into my mouth and deepening the kiss.

I tear my mouth from hers, trailing my lips down her neck, nipping on the sensitive skin as I cup her breasts, my thumbs finding her nipples through the material of her t-shirt. She arches her back, pushing her glorious tits against my hands as I stroke her nipples to hard nubs and she gasps my name.

"I missed you," I growl, pulling back to look into her green eyes, now hooded with desire.

"So I noticed," she says, breathlessly. "You can miss me as often as you like if that's the kind of hello I get."

I lean in to kiss her softly. "Much as I'd like to strip you naked and screw you senseless right now. I need to get you down the station."

"Spoilsport!" Trish jokes, pushing her bottom lip out and I can't resist biting it gently, immediately soothing the area with my tongue.

I force myself to step away from the temptation of her body, trying to control the demands of my body while she grabs her purse and keys before we head out to the car.

"So, are you officially part of the police force again now?" Trish asks once we're on the road.

"Technically, I was never off the force, but during my time UC, I had a whole new identity, a fabricated criminal record, the works. It had to look convincing."

"UC?" Trish queries.

"Sorry, police lingo. It means under cover."

"Ah, of course. Aren't you worried that they'll find you now your cover's blown?" Her brow creases with worry at the thought.

"Going UC is always a risk, Trish, but it's a risk I was willing to take a year ago. Now, maybe not so much. I had less to lose back then." I reach across and link my fingers through hers, keeping my other hand on the wheel.

Trish looks at me with her heart in her eyes and it's all I can do to keep the car in a straight line. "I don't know what I'd do if anything happened to you," she whispers and I can see the sheen of tears in her beautiful green eyes.

"Nothing's going to happen to me, honey. There are lots of measures put into place so that my real identity isn't exposed. My handler is one of only a few people who knew my real name. It keeps everyone safe," I reassure her.

"Your handler?"

"A handler is your point of contact. The one person you report back to, who keeps you grounded and reminds you who you are, what your mission is," I explain. "That's one of the biggest problems - making sure you don't get psychologically mixed up in what you're doing and forget who you really are."

"You don't strike me as the kind of person who would allow yourself to do that," Trish says. "You're too focused, too self-aware."

"That's a deep observation." Her perception always surprises me and shoot her an admiring look. "I was only UC for a year. Lev Sarado, my handler, was UC for almost eight years. He had to do things that most of us have nightmares about, like lines of cocaine when gang bosses were hosting parties, just to maintain his cover. He found it tough reintegrating and spent a lot of time with the force psychologist afterward."

"What a sacrifice to make for the greater good," Trish says, sympathetically. "I know that what happened yesterday wasn't ideal, but in a way, I'm glad because the thought of you living that life for eight years, the danger you'd be in every day, scares me."

"Part of the reason I went UC was because my parents were killed in a car wreck when I was in my early twenties," I confide, hearing Trish's sharp intake of breath at my revelation. "It was an eighteen-year-old kid who was high on cocaine. He got behind the wheel and hit my parents head-on at an intersection. I was just finishing my cadet training at the academy. That's when I swore I would do whatever I could to make a difference, so that no other kids have to lose their parents and no parents have to lose their eighteen-year-old son."

"I'm so sorry, Daryl! I can't imagine how devastating that must have been," Trish says quietly, squeezing my hand tighter, her eyes full of horror at my loss. "It seems like we've both been the unwilling victims of drugs in different ways," she says sadly.

"Ain't that the truth, honey," I say, pulling up in front of the station and cutting the engine.

Once inside, I get Trish signed in and give her a visitor's badge before leading her through to the main office which is bustling with activity. A few of my old colleagues I haven't seen for almost a year call out to me, stopping to shake hands and welcome me back, casting curious glances at Trish.

I grin as a tall, stocky guy with blond hair approaches and we shake hands. "Hey, Tony."

"Good to have you back, partner," Tony says.

"It's good to be back. I missed your ugly face."

"Hey, now. Is that any way to greet your old friend?" Tony pretends to be insulted before turning his gaze to Trish. "I don't believe we've had the pleasure." Instead of shaking the hand that Trish raises, he lifts it to his lips and I resist the urge to yank her hand away.

"Tony, this is Trish. Trish, meet the asshole that is my partner," I say, smirking at my friend.

"Enchanté, Trish." Tony bows and kisses the tips of her fingers. "Pleasure to meet you. And what, may I ask, is a lovely woman such as yourself, doing with a reprobate like him?" Tony jerks his thumb in my direction.

Trish laughs. "Ah, you know. He's got that whole tall, dark and dangerous thing going on," she jokes.

Tony feigns a hurt expression. "I knew it! Always the bridesmaid, never the bride, when this guy is around. Well, Trish, if you ever need a little light relief from the tall, dark and dangerous vibe he likes to give out, I do a great tall, blond and insanely funny."

53

Trish grins. "I'll bear that in mind, Tony."

Tony turns back to me. "Seriously, D. It's good to have you back," he says, using the nickname he gave me back in the day.

"Good to be back, Tony." I clap the other man on the back as he turns to leave.

"He seems nice," Trish says, as I steer her through to a private office.

"He's a good man," I reply. "I've known Tony a long time. We went through the academy together. He was there for me when I lost my parents. He knew them too and was almost as devastated as I was."

"I'm glad you had someone looking out for you," Trish says softly, reaching for my hand and squeezing it.

I bring her hand to my mouth, opening her fingers and placing a kiss against her palm, my tongue darting out to taste her soft skin. Her eyes catch fire at the small caress and the world stops for a minute, my vision narrowing to the woman in front of me as everything else fades away.

The sound of a phone ringing breaks the spell and I release Trish's hand reluctantly, pulling out a chair and indicating for her to sit at the desk in front of the computer. I lean in behind her as I log into the system, the floral scent that is uniquely her drifting over me and making me instantly hard.

"You just need to scroll through the records, like this," I say, showing her what to do. "If you see anyone or anything familiar, anything at all, just give me a shout. I'll go grab you a coffee - you're going to need it."

I, on the other hand, may need a shot of something stronger to keep my hands off her.

Two hours later, Trish is no nearer to identifying Salvadore and it's beginning to feel like looking for the proverbial needle in a haystack.

Trish sits back in her chair, stretching her stiff muscles and my eyes drop to her chest as her movements pull her t-shirt taut across her generous tits. "I'm sorry, Daryl, but I haven't seen anyone that looks like the man I saw that night."

"It's okay, honey. There's no guarantee he's even in our database. We're probably clutching at straws but it was worth a try."

Trish becomes quiet, lost in thought for a minute. "There is one other thing we could try, that I could try."

I raise my eyebrows questioningly, wondering where her train of thought is leading.

She takes a deep breath. "I think it's time I paid Pete a visit."

TRISH

I'm pretty sure I've lost my mind, offering to visit my ex-husband, a man I haven't seen since he was he was sent to prison. The thought of going to see him now terrifies me, but something tells me it's the right thing to do. Pete must have evidence on who Salvadore is - it's the only explanation for why he's still drawing breath. Like Daryl said yesterday, Salvadore has had people killed for less than the sins Pete committed against him.

I sigh, feeling like I've stumbled into some television police drama. Who knew how complicated my life would become because of a man I married when I was barely eighteen years old?

Daryl perches on the edge of the desk next to me, resting his hands on his jean clad thighs, his proximity making it difficult to concentrate when all I want to do is climb into his lap and rub myself against him.

"I appreciate what you're trying to do, Trish, but are you really prepared for that? Seeing the man who was responsible for so much pain?" Daryl asks, frowning.

"If it means putting an end to all this, then yes. I can't keep living my life under this shadow. I know Pete wouldn't tell you anything, but maybe I can convince him, if not for my sake then for the sake of his daughter. It has to be worth a try. At least then, I'll know I did everything I could to finally put all this to rest."

Daryl leans forward, capturing my eyes with his. "Are you sure about this? Nailing Salvadore is important but not as important as your safety. Not to me."

"I'm sure," I whisper, touched by Daryl's words and wondering what the hell I've just committed myself to.

"Okay. I'll set it up, but on the condition that I come with you. You're not doing this alone."

Half an hour later, we're back at my apartment and I walk straight through to the kitchen, intending to make us both coffee. I reach two cups down from the cupboard and as I turn to place them on the worktop, I find Daryl standing right behind me.

Before I can speak his mouth comes crashing down on mine and the touch of his lips lights the touch-paper of my ever-present desire for him. Our kiss becomes desperate, hungry, as he devours my mouth with his, our tongues sparring in an age-old dance of lust.

"God, Trish, I'm on fucking fire for you. I've been dreaming about your hands on me, burying myself inside you ever since I left here yesterday."

I moan at Daryl's words, so hot for him that I want nothing more than the feel of him inside me, filling me to the brim with his steely length. I reach for the buttons of his jeans with frenzied hands, pushing them down his hips along with his boxers and wrapping my fingers greedily around his swollen shaft.

I sweep my fingers around his engorged length, cupping my hands around his balls, finding sensitive spot underneath and making him jerk uncontrollably as my fingers stroke back and forth.

"Dear God, Trish! You're driving me fucking insane, woman. I want inside baby, I need to fuck you hard!"

His words are a growl as his hands go to my skirt, tugging it up around my waist and tugging my panties out of the way as he lifts me onto the worktop. He pulls my butt roughly to the edge of the counter, his hands moving to press my thighs apart as he positions me and impales me with one smooth thrust of his hips.

"Oh, God, Daryl! That feels so good!" I moan.

A part of me can't believe he's fucking me on the edge of my kitchen worktop, while another part of me revels in the knowledge of how hot this is, his overwhelming desire for me reflected in the roughness of his movements.

I brace my hands behind me as I wrap my legs around his hips, holding him to me as he pounds in and out of me, our bodies slapping together in a fierce rhythm. My head falls back as I feel my climax building from the friction of him against my clit with each thrust of his hips.

I hear a keening sound and realise it's coming from me, utterly lost to the strength of my orgasm as it bites into my body and I shout my release. Daryl follows close behind, his fingers bruising my thighs as he rivets himself to me, choking out his climax as he fills me to the brim with his hot cum.

We're both gasping for breath after our frantic sex and I slowly become aware of our surroundings again, feeling the cold surface of the worktop under my butt.

Daryl lifts his head from my shoulder, his eyes questioning as he feels my body shaking with laughter. "What's so funny?"

"I'm just thinking I'll need to make sure I steri-wipe the kitchen worktop!" I choke, and Daryl grins at my infectious laughter.

"Yeah. Probably best to do that before we make anything to eat," he chuckles, leaning forward to kiss me gently before lowering me down from the worktop and bending to pull up his boxers and jeans. We were in such a hurry we only managed to get the necessary clothing out of the way.

I feel his warm fluids trickle between my thighs, a reminder of the passion we've just shared but before I can head to the bathroom to clean up, Daryl scoops up my discarded panties, using them to gently wipe me clean in an intimacy I've never experienced, before bringing them to his nose and inhaling deeply.

I flush, finding the sight both embarrassing and hot at the same time. "I'm having so many firsts with you," I murmur, moving into the circle of his arms and looking up at him. "I never dreamed, in all my wildest fantasies, that sex could be like this."

Daryl spears his fingers through my hair, tipping my head back so he can kiss me deeply and slowly, his lips teasing mine. "Me, either. Everything just feels right with you. All my

59

inhibitions go out the window every time I put my hands on you."

"It's the same for me," I sigh. "Sex with Pete was always a quick affair and he never really cared about my pleasure as long as he got his." I pause, looking at Daryl. "Sex with you is a million miles away from anything Pete and I ever shared. It's mind-blowing."

"You think sex with me is mind-blowing, wait until I've cooked for you," Daryl growls, nipping my mouth.

"You're going to cook for me?"

"Yep. You go freshen up and I'll run out and get the ingredients. Do you like spaghetti?"

My stomach growls in answer and I grin.

Once Daryl's gone, I take a quick shower, feeling happier than I can ever remember, despite the spectre of Salvadore and my upcoming visit to see Pete hanging over us. It's going to be very strange seeing my ex-husband after almost ten years and I'm glad that Daryl is coming with me for moral support.

I dress quickly in leggings and a t-shirt, pulling my hair up into a loose ponytail and heading back to the kitchen to make the coffee I intended to make earlier, my face heating as I remember what that had led to.

Daryl returns shortly after and it's not long before the delicious smell of spaghetti bolognese and garlic bread is permeating my apartment. We sit down to eat at the small dining table and I can't remember a time when I felt more content, more alive.

"Oh, my God, this is delicious!" I moan around a mouthful of the rich bolognese. "You're right, your cooking skills are even more mind-blowing than the sex," I tease, waggling my eyebrows at Daryl.

"I'm going to take great pleasure in hearing you take that back later," Daryl pins me with a hot stare and I feel my whole body heat up under his gaze.

"Promises, promises," I murmur, smiling at him as I take a bite of the garlic bread, watching his eyes lower hungrily to my mouth as the butter from the bread coats my lips. "So, what happens tomorrow?" I ask, needing to know what to expect.

Daryl swallows a mouthful of spaghetti before answering. "I've filed a visiting application for you and cleared us for a visit tomorrow afternoon. You still determined to do this?"

I nod, knowing that our choices are limited. "Yeah. It's just going to be weird seeing Pete after so long, you know? I haven't wanted any contact with him since everything went to shit. Even if he can't tell us anymore than we already know, maybe it will at least help me to face old demons and finally put the past to rest."

Daryl reaches across the table and twines his fingers with mine. "Whichever way it goes it's all good, Trish. I just want you to know how much I appreciate you trying. I know how difficult all of this is for you. I've given you a lot to absorb over the last twenty-four hours and you've taken it all in your stride and then some. It just proves what an amazingly strong woman you are."

"Hush now, you've made me spring a leak," I joke, fighting back tears at his words.

Daryl pushes his chair back and stands and I look up as he approaches me. His eyes bore into mine with singular intent as he pulls me to my feet, our food forgotten as he leads me into the bedroom.

He stops next to the bed and begins to slowly strip, removing his t-shirt while I eat him up with my eyes, loving the hard muscles that are such a contrast to my own softer curves. His hands go to the buttons of his jeans and they join his discarded t-shirt on the floor along with his boxers shorts until he's completely naked in front of me, his erect shaft standing out proudly from his body, the end glistening with pre-cum.

"Take your clothes off," he instructs, and the demand makes my heart pound with anticipation.

I reach for the hem of my t-shirt, giving him the same show he's just given me as I tug it over my head and remove my bra. His eyes land on my breasts and my nipples harden, my back arching involuntarily as my body seeks his touch, his mouth. I slide my leggings and panties down and kick them off, already feeling the moisture pooling between my legs.

I climb onto the bed, moving to lie in the middle and let my knees drop open, loving the sound of his groan as his hot gaze rests on my glistening pussy.

I moan, instinctively lifting my hips off the bed as I feel the weight of his eyes on me, lighting fires wherever they land.

Daryl settles his weight on the bed, positioning himself between my thighs and his hands press my knees further apart as he leans forward, pressing the end of his shaft against my wet opening. His big body cages me in as he skims his hands up my sides to cup my breasts, dipping his head to pull a nipple into his mouth and suckle me while his fingers pinch my other nipple.

I arch off the bed toward his mouth, a pool of warmth spiralling through my stomach and landing in a needy pulse between my thighs as his mouth moves to lavish the same attention on my other nipple. I shift restlessly on the bed, on fire as I writhe underneath him, seeking a closer contact with his hard body.

His lips feather down my stomach as he licks and nips at my skin until his mouth hovers over my mound. "Do you want my mouth on you, Trish? My tongue on your clit, sucking you until you cum?"

Dear God, does he really need an answer to that? I moan, lifting my hips towards his mouth in mute answer and cry out as I feel his warm tongue sliding between my cleft, opening me up to his mouth as he finds my clit and suckles me there just like he did with my nipples minutes ago.

"Oh, God, Daryl. I didn't know it would feel so good!" I moan.

Daryl pauses and looks up at me in surprise. "You've never had anyone go down on you before?"

"Never," I breathe. "Don't stop, please!"

"Oh, I won't stop, honey. Not until you scream my name and coat my mouth with your juices," he promises and his tongue finds my sensitive nub again, flicking back and forth as he works me toward my orgasm.

Maintaining the rhythm with his mouth and tongue, he slips a finger inside me, hooking it around to find my sweet spot and the pressure of his finger and his tongue has me flying over the edge.

"Daryl!" I scream his name as my orgasm buffets me and my juices gush into his mouth, just as he promised a moment ago. My hips arch off the bed as my hands tangle in his hair, holding him to me as I eke the last spasms of pleasure from my climax, never wanting it to end.

It takes me a while to catch my breath after one of the most amazing releases of my life and I once again wonder at my body's seemingly endless desire for this man, knowing that it's born of more than just a physical attraction.

I pull him up to me, kissing him deeply and tasting my love juices on his mouth. "Thank you," I say, feeling a tear slip from the corner of my eye.

Daryl bends to kiss it away, his lips feathering over my brow, my cheeks, teasing my lips as he nudges my legs apart, looking into my eyes as he positions himself and slowly, slowly merges his body with mine. His hips lift away and I moan at the loss but it's short-lived as submerges himself fully within my tight channel with a powerful thrust, burying himself so deeply that I know he's branded me forever his.

"Trish, you feel so fucking good!" he moans, increasing the tempo of his hips. He grabs my thighs, tilting me slightly to allow him to penetrate even deeper, his shaft bottoming out inside me with every thrust of his body.

"Fuck me hard, Daryl," I moan, biting his shoulder, and my words splinter his control as he pounds his body into mine, driving toward his own orgasm.

"Oh, God, Trish! I'm gonna cum, baby!" I watch, fascinated, as he throws his head back and roars at the force of his climax, grinding his hips into me as he rides the last of his pleasure before collapsing on top of me.

I keep my legs wrapped around him, still holding him inside me, even when I feel his warm seed trickling out of me and between my ass cheeks. I don't want to relinquish this closeness, not just yet.

Our breathing slowly returns to normal and Daryl rolls us onto our sides, our bodies still intimately joined. "Just when I think it can't get any better, *that* happens," he chuckles, nuzzling my neck.

I stroke his sweaty hair back from his forehead, languishing in the simple pleasure of being with him, feeling his heart beating against mine and the warmth of his breath whispering over my skin.

"I want you this close to me every night," I say, taking a deep breath as I know that what I'm about to admit will give him all the power. "I love you, Daryl. I think I fell in love with you the minute you walked into the diner." I hold my breath, waiting for his response and unable to lift my eyes to his in case all I see in them is rejection.

His fingers come under my chin, tilting my face up so that our eyes collide. "I love you too, baby, from the moment I saw your picture in your file. You're more than I could ever have dreamed of, ever hoped for and when this whole thing with Salvadore is done, I want to make things permanent between us. I want a ring on your finger and I want the whole fucking world to know you're mine."

I throw my arms around him, holding him to me as happiness bubbles up inside me, flooding through my bloodstream and making me giddy.

Daryl laughs, hugging me back just as tightly. "Is that a yes?"

"Yes, yes, yes!" I kiss him with each 'yes' and we lie in each other's arms, touching and kissing softly until my eyelids droop closed and sleep overtakes me.

I'm back in my old house, standing at the top of the stairs as I try to make out what the voices coming from the kitchen are saying. I know Pete's voice well, but the deep husk of the other male voice is unfamiliar to me.

What the hell is someone doing here at this time of the night?

I slink back into the shadows as a man emerges from the kitchen. I can't see his face as his back is to me and he's wearing a long, black coat that looks to be made of pure wool, his shoes polished to a high shine. This is a man with expensive tastes. He's a big man, maybe six four with broad shoulders and blond hair.

As he leaves, he pulls up the collar of his coat against the chill wind and I notice that the end of his right pinkie finger is missing at the first knuckle......

I jolt awake at the memory, my subconscious mind having recovered the small detail that my waking mind had dismissed at the time.

Daryl's body is wrapped around mine from behind, one hand cupping my breast, his breathing steady and peaceful and I can't bring myself to disturb him.

Plenty of time to tell him what I've remembered tomorrow, I think, as sleep claims me again.

DARYL

The vibration of my cell on the bedside cabinet wakes me and I gently disentangle myself from Trish without waking her, rolling over to check the caller ID.

It's two in the morning and Lev has left several text messages, asking me to call him, so it must be something urgent.

I get out of bed, careful not to disturb Trish and head through to the living room, closing the bedroom door behind me.

"What's up?" I ask, as Lev answers my call on the first ring.

"Some new developments." Lev's voice is serious. "A member of Salvadore's inner circle is willing to come forward with some evidence that could wrap up this whole case."

"What? Why now?" I ask, hardly daring to believe that our luck has turned.

"It seems he got wind of what happened with Guillermo and feels it's in his...best interests to cooperate with us in exchange for protection. Thing is, he'll only deal with you. Says you're the man to bring Salvadore down. Any idea why he might say that?"

"None. Unless it's because he knows I took out two of Salvadore's men. Which means my identity is no longer a secret," I state. "Shit! If that's the case then it changes everything. We definitely have a leak."

"If our informant knows your real identity then you can bet that Salvadore does too," Lev points out. "What about your partner, Tony? Do you trust him?"

"Are you serious? I've known him for more than twenty years. There's no way he could be mixed up in something like this. Besides, he knows I was UC but he's completely in the dark about the case and my cover, for his own protection, as well as mine."

"Okay, okay. Calm down. I'm just trying to consider all options here. The redhead, Trish, was it? Do you trust her? Maybe she's more involved that we think. After all, her ex-husband was balls-deep in Salvadore's operation. Is it possible she has connections of her own?"

"No way," I say, adamantly. "She didn't even know about Salvadore until two days ago and tomorrow will be the first time she's had any kind of contact with her ex-husband for almost ten years."

"When she goes to the prison?"

"Yeah. She's prepared to go through with it if it means we can get Salvadore's real identity. Pete's own testimony may not be worth shit, but if he has the hard evidence we think he does and she can talk him into sharing it, it could be just what we need to end this."

Lev sighs down the phone. "Okay, but you need to meet with the informant tomorrow afternoon. He's going to call me an hour before with a time and place."

"Fuck! I promised I'd go with her," I explode, not happy at the change of plans and quickly trying to come up with another solution. "Tony can take her. I'll brief him tomorrow morning."

"Okay, good. That way we keep both options open. Trish goes to see Pete, you meet up with the informant and we hope that something concrete comes from one of those meetings."

I still don't feel happy about not going with Trish, but I know she'll be safe with Tony. "Okay. I'll wait to hear from you with a time and place."

I end the call and drop my head into my hands, running my fingers through my hair in agitation. I have a gut feeling that something isn't right. It's tugging at my brain but I can't quite grasp it. I should be pleased that we have two avenues open to us that could potentially nail Salvadore but part of me can't quite believe it's that easy.

I lean back against the sofa with a weary sigh. What is it they say about not looking a gift horse in the mouth? Part of working a case is waiting and hoping for a break like this, isn't it? I force down the uncertain feeling, my tired brain not wanting to analyse it any further right now.

I climb back into bed and Trish curls her warm body against mine, murmuring in her sleep. I nuzzle my face into her curls and kiss her forehead lightly, holding her to me as I allow the comfort I find in her arms to wash over me, soothing me back to sleep.

TRISH

It's late when I wake the next morning. Daryl is gone again and I sigh, already missing the feel of his body against mine.

I take a quick shower, washing and drying my hair before dressing in black pants and a green sweater. The weather is unseasonably chilly today and I know I'll appreciate the extra warmth.

Daryl has left me another note which I pull from the front of the kitchen cupboard.

Sorry, honey, something important came up regarding the case which means I won't be able to go with you this afternoon. Tony will pick you up at 1pm and take to you the prison. I'll call you later. Love you.

I'm disappointed that Daryl won't be coming with me but I know that the information must be crucial if he's been called away. His declaration of love at the end of his note warms me and reassures me that last night wasn't just a dream. That thought suddenly reminds me of my dream and that I need to contact him to tell him what I've remembered about Salvadore.

Grabbing my phone, I call his number but it goes straight to answerphone so I leave a message with the information in the hope that it may be helpful.

No sooner have I ended the call than my phone lights up with Barbara's number.

"Hey, Barb."

"Hi there, honey. How are you?" The sound of Barb's familiar voice is comforting.

"I'm good, thanks. Is everything okay at the diner? Is Helena covering my shifts?" I ask.

"Yes, and yes," Barb laughs. "Don't worry, honey, everything is under control. Are you really doing okay?"

"I guess it's stirred up a lot of bad memories," I admit. "One of the guys they arrested yesterday was the brother of Diego Martinez."

"Oh, my goodness! What are the chances?" Barb sounds shocked at my revelations.

I hesitate, wondering how much I should say to Barb but needing to confide in someone. Who better than my friend and one of the people I trust most in the world?

I tell Barb everything, about Salvadore and Daryl's suspicions that Pete has the evidence needed to take him down as well as my planned visit to the prison to see him.

"I can't believe it!" Barb exclaims. "Come to think, it was a bit odd because I expected the diner to be crawling with police for days, but nothing. No one's been back since they left on Tuesday. Almost like the whole thing's been hushed up."

"I know what you mean," I agree, as Barb echoes my own thoughts of a few evenings ago.

"Are you sure? About going to see Pete, I mean?" Barb's voice is full of concern.

"I've got to, Barb," I sigh. "It just seems like my past won't stay in my past. I need to see this through to the end. I couldn't live with myself if I had the opportunity to end all this and I didn't take it. I don't think Prue and I can really have any peace of mind until it's done and if it means we can take down Salvadore at the same time then it has to be worth it."

"Oh, honey, I'm so sorry you're going through all this again!" Barb says, her voice full of sympathy. "I remember how broken you were when you came to live with me after you left Pete, after Prue was...." her voice trails off, both of us knowing what she was going to say.

After Prue was almost raped.

Barb had been our saviour when Prue and I left Pete and I'll never be able to repay the debt of her kindness during that time. The older woman has become a mother figure to me over the years, she and her husband never having had kids of their own. She lost her beloved Henry almost twelve years ago to a heart attack.

"Prue and I owe you a lot, Barb. You were there for us when we had nothing." I can feel the sting of tears at the back of my eyes.

"I'm just glad I was able to help, honey," Barb says softly. "You and Prue are family."

"We feel the same," I say, my throat thick with tears.

"Okay, now you're gonna make me cry too!" Barb sniffs. "Listen, honey. It's Friday tomorrow and Helena has already said she can cover so I don't want to see you back here until Monday, okay? We'll work out the money side of things then. You need to concentrate on this business with Pete. Just promise me you'll be careful and tell Daryl if anything happens to my girl, I'll string him up by his balls!"

I laugh at Barb's words, dashing away the tears that are threatening to fall. "I'll tell him. I think he may be more scared of you than the guy he's going after!"

"It doesn't hurt to threaten them with a little pain every now and again to make them toe the line," Barb chuckles.

We chat for a few minutes more before we end the call, with me promising I'll see Barb on Monday.

I check the clock on the kitchen wall and realize that I only have forty-five minutes before Tony picks me up. I make myself some brunch, noticing for the first time that Daryl must have cleared away our dishes from last night and I smile to myself - any guy who cleans up after himself is definitely a keeper.

After demolishing a cheese omelette and salad, I debate whether I have time to call Prue, maybe catch her in her lunch hour. Part of me really wants to talk to her before I visit Pete but my protective instincts can't risk that she'll pick up something in my voice, sensitive as we are to each other's moods. I can always call her later or tomorrow, depending on how things go today.

At one pm prompt, there's a knock at the door, and I quickly check my appearance before going to answer it.

"Hey, Trish." Tony grins at me from the doorway.

"Hi, Tony. Thanks for stepping in for Daryl." I return his grin.

"No problem," Tony replies. "Any excuse to get away from the mountain of paperwork on my desk."

"I guess that's a big part of your job nowadays," I say, sympathetically, grabbing my coat and closing the door behind me as I follow Tony to the car, an unmarked Dodge Charger.

"Like you wouldn't believe," Tony groans, holding the passenger door open while I climb in.

I settle myself in the seat, my eyes drawn to the multitude of electronic gadgets as I buckle up. "Nice car," I say, as Tony climbs in next to me.

"V6 and V8 engines with 292 and 370 HP respectively. Integrated twelve-inch display with keyboard connected to a trunk-mounted computer, UConnect 5 and seven-inch color-customizable instrument gauge cluster. Oh, and electric steering wheel," Tony reels off.

"Oookay. You could have been talking Yurdish for all the sense that made to me. I actually just meant that I like the color!" I laugh.

"Yurdish? Is that even a real language?" Tony chuckles. "Anyway, what is it with women and car color?"

"Well, it's one of the most important considerations when choosing a car," I argue, tongue-in-cheek.

"Yeah, because God forbid if it doesn't match the colour of the fluffy dice and seat covers," Tony agrees, winking at me.

I laugh, the banter with Tony easing my nerves a little at the prospect of what lies ahead.

"So, you ready for this?" he asks, as if reading my mind.

"I'll never be ready for it, Tony," I reply, clasping my hands nervously in my lap. "But, if it helps to get Salvadore then it'll be worth it."

"You're a brave woman," Tony says, casting me an admiring glance. "You could've just walked away from all this. Why didn't you?"

"To help Daryl. And because there's a part of me that needs the closure, I just didn't realize it until two days ago. If nothing else, I think seeing Pete will give me that."

"Well, let's hope he gives you that and more," Tony says, looking more serious than I've ever seen him in the short time I've known him. He strikes me as the happy-go-lucky type, but I wonder if there is a more serious side underneath his sunny personality.

We fall into a comfortable silence and I settle back, watching the built-up skylines drop away as we head through the tunnel that takes us out of town and into the more rural areas.

The journey passes surprisingly quickly and it's not long before we're driving through the prison gates. The main red-brick building sits in the middle of the prison complex surrounded by twenty-foot-high barbed wire fences. The building has four turret structures on each corner and various annexes running off it and I wonder which of those areas has been Pete's home for the last ten years.

After parking in the visitor's parking lot, Tony and I head to the processing center where I fill out the necessary paperwork and undergo a search before being issued with a pass. This is all foreign me and I can't help wishing that Daryl were with despite Tony being good company.

"Good luck, Trish," Tony says, as my name is called and I follow a mountain of a man with graying hair toward the visiting room.

I feel the nervous sweat breaking out on my palms as we approach the door. The man directs me to a small table with a curt nod of his head and I take a seat in one of the two chairs, my stomach churning as the reality of what I'm doing descends on me.

I glance around, noticing there are several other visitors waiting at tables just like mine, some already with their loved ones. I wonder briefly what their stories are, the path their lives have taken them down that led them here. Maybe they're wondering the same about me as I sit waiting for the ex-husband who almost destroyed my life, my daughter's life.

A movement from the corner of the room catches my eye as a door opens and a man is escorted into the room.

It takes me a full minute to recognise Pete. He seems to have shrunk over the years, his previously thick, sandy hair has thinned and is now liberally sprinkled with gray. The handsome face that used to be wrinkle free now shows signs of premature aging, the rigors of his life and drug abuse having carved deep lines into his forehead and around his eyes.

He takes the seat across from me and our eyes meet for the first time in almost ten years, his watery blue gaze falling on my face as he gives me the same appraisal I just subjected him to.

"Hello, Trish. You look good." His voice is just as I remember, unleashing all kinds of memories and it upsets me that so few of them are happy.

"Hello, Pete." I can't bring myself to tell him he looks good because that would be a lie.

"What? Not gonna return the compliment?" He says with a wry smile, as if reading my thoughts. "Never mind, don't answer that. I know time hasn't been kind to this ugly mug, unlike you. You look exactly like you did when we were fifteen, Trish."

I grimace. "A lot older and a lot wiser now, Pete. That was a long time ago and there's been a lot of water under the bridge since then."

Pete leans forward, resting his elbows on the table in front of him. "We had some good times though, didn't we, Trish? In the beginning?"

I sigh, not in the mood for a walk down memory lane, but knowing I have to play it cool if I have any chance of getting the information we want. "We did. But we were both so young, Pete. We should never have gotten married. You and I, what we had, was never strong enough for forever. The very best thing that came out of our relationship was Prue, and I'll never regret having her."

Pete's expression closes up at the mention of our daughter. "How is she?"

"Damaged," I say bluntly, struggling to keep my voice even. "What did you expect, Pete? That she'd skip happily away from what happened, what you almost allowed to happen?"

Pete looks at me and I see genuine remorse, the pain in his eyes that of a tortured soul looking for redemption for his actions and finding none. "I will never forgive myself for what happened that day, Trish. And not just that day, but every other day that I was at the mercy of my habit. I know you don't want to hear any of this but the drugs changed me, made me self-absorbed, weak. I didn't care about anyone or anything except where my next fix was coming from. And the whole time, I was going to great lengths to hide it all from you, from Prue."

77

"I can't believe I didn't see what was going on under my nose. What was right in front of my face," I whisper. I should have known, should've seen the signs. Maybe then I could have gotten you the help you needed and things would have been different." I dash away the tear that trickles down my cheek.

"You have absolutely nothing to blame yourself for, Trish," Pete reaches across as if to place his hand over mine before hesitating, curling his fingers back in on themselves. "I made my own choices, I'm responsible for my own fuck-ups, but to my everlasting shame, I brought you and Prue along for the ride, and for that I will be eternally sorry."

Pete pauses, clasping his hands together on the table in front of him. "I'm paying my dues, Trish, and it's no less than I deserve." He looks directly at me. "But you don't need to pay them with me. Seems like you've locked yourself in a prison of your own making and it's time you set yourself free."

Pete has just reiterated what Prue has been telling me for years but hearing the words directly from him loosens some of the deep-rooted guilt I've carried for so long, allowing it to float away like negative energy dispersing into the ether.

"Thank you," I whisper, feeling a lightness that I haven't felt for years. I didn't think Pete had anything of value left to give me, but he's just proved me wrong with those words.

"I went through a detox program here," Pete continues, "and I've found some measure of salvation in God, in the hope that He will grant me forgiveness and that maybe, one day, you and Prue will too."

"I'm glad you've found some peace, Pete," I say, surprised that I genuinely mean my words, "but Prue and I are still searching for ours. We're still dealing with the consequences of your actions to this day. It's the reason I'm here."

"Ah, so now we get to the crux of the matter," Pete smiles knowingly. "Let me guess. You're here because you want to know Salvadore's identity. I take it that Daryl Jacobs has been talking to you?"

"How did you...?"

"Because he's been here. Asking me questions. None of which I was prepared to answer beyond what they already know. I won't have you and Prue put in harm's way again, Trish. I was hoping that you'd never have to get involved in all this, that you could both get on with your lives, even though it meant I'd never see you or my daughter again, but I can see that isn't the case, or you wouldn't be here."

"I am involved, Pete, because I'm involved with Daryl."

I can see that Pete understands my meaning immediately and he nods, as if I've just confirmed something that he already knew. "Daryl seems like a good man. I'm happy for you. I know he'll look after you, Trish."

"He *is* a good man, Pete, which is why I have to help him." I tell Pete everything that's happened over the last few days, from inadvertently stumbling upon the meeting with Guillermo to Daryl's belief that I can identify Salvadore.

"Shit!" Pete leans back in his chair, rubbing his hands across his face. "I never meant for you to be in this situation, Trish. I had ... insurance against Salvadore, something that meant he couldn't lay a finger on me without exposing himself, his real identity. Of course, I was so fucked up on drugs at the time that it never occurred to me that he would target my family instead, that he would harm our daughter, an innocent girl."

"Was it him that came to the house that night?" I ask.

"Yes, it was him. I knew he was on to me so I sent word out, knowing it would reach him, making it clear that I had

79

evidence that could expose him if he ever came after me. The night you saw him was the night he decided to pay me a visit - he wanted to meet the man who thought he had the balls big enough to take him on."

Pete laughs humorlessly. "I thought I was such a fucking big-shot, that I had it all under control. He left that night, and I thought I'd won. I should have known it wasn't that simple. My enormous ego couldn't contemplate that he would send Diego Martinez to teach me a lesson. It's a lesson I've been reliving every day of my life since. It's why I didn't run when you called the cops, because I deserve every single day of the punishment that was dealt out to me and more."

"But, if you've known his identity all along, why haven't you exposed him before now?"

"Because my testimony won't count for shit as long as I've got a hole in my ass, Trish. I blew any credibility I had the day I snorted my first line. Plus, I had a feeling the evidence might still have some future value and I didn't want to play my hand too early. There was only ever one person I would reveal the evidence to and that person is sitting in front of me. You're the only person that I knew would use it for the right reasons. So, I've been waiting for you to come here and ask me but hoping that you never would because it would mean that you've been pulled into my fucking mess yet again."

"You're going to tell me what you have on him?" I whisper.

"No, because *I* don't have anything on him, Trish." Pete looks me straight in the eye. "But *you* do."

DARYL

I spend the morning briefing Tony, catching him up on the case and reconnecting with my friend after almost a year UC. We settle easily back into our familiar partnership and I realize how much I've missed his light-hearted banter and positive attitude. It's why we work so well together - he's the perfect complement to my more serious nature.

"Don't worry, D," Tony says, when I ask him to accompany Trish to the prison. "I'll make sure she gets there okay."

"Thanks, Tony. I wish I could go myself but I'm the only one the informant will talk to," I sigh. "I just hope it's worth it."

"Go do what you gotta do. I'll take care of everything here," Tony reassures me.

Just before midday, I receive the phone call I've been waiting for from Lev, giving me the time and place for the meeting. It's about an hour out of town in a rural area and I arrive ten minutes early, giving me the opportunity to scope out my surroundings.

Forty minutes later I'm beginning to wonder what the fuck I'm doing here. I've been cooling my heels waiting for a man it appears isn't going to show and I'm pissed - I hate having my time wasted especially today when I could've been with Trish.

The rendezvous point is a crossroads on the outskirts of town. The rural location means I haven't been able to get a signal on my cell since I arrived so I haven't even been able to contact Lev to find out where the fuck our man is. Despite that, I must admit it's certainly a better spot than Guillermo's choice of meeting place.

Why had he wanted to meet in the alley? Only now, I recall his words of two days ago.

How do you think I knew you were a cop?

I haven't given his words much thought, caught up as I've been with Trish, but now I'm pissed at myself for not taking those words more seriously.

Guillermo had known I was a cop, which meant that he'd never had any intention of going through with the drop. So, why had he been there? What could he have possibly gained from the set-up? Was it to expose me? But to what end?

The fact that Guillermo had known I was a cop also meant that someone had blown my cover. Someone I trusted. Someone I thought had my back.

My mind is in overdrive now, rapidly processing snippets of information and fragments of memory and suddenly everything comes into sharp focus.

Guillermo had wanted the meeting in the alley behind the diner because he'd figured out who my potential witness was, the one person who might be able to identify his boss. No one except Peter Townley and myself had known that it was Trish, so how had he found out? Right up until a few days before, another operative had been lined up to investigate Trish, but I'd pulled a few strings to take that responsibility for myself. Or had I? Had someone else been pulling the strings all along?

I can't believe how fucking stupid I've been, how blind! I pace away from the car, running my hands through my hair, trying to make all the pieces fit together.

As I walk, my phone vibrates in my pocket and I pull it out to see I have one bar, having obviously hit a hotspot with my pacing. I stay rooted to the spot so as not to lose the signal, tapping in my code to see I have a missed call from Trish along with an answerphone message.

"Hey. It's me. Um, sorry you can't come with me today but I understand why. I remembered something last night, when I fell asleep. Something about the man who came to the house that night. I don't know if it will help, if it even means anything but he, uh, he had part of his little finger missing on his right hand. Silly, I know, but I thought it was worth mentioning. Anyway, I'm going soon so, uh, I'll see you later? I love you."

Jesus Christ! My stomach turns over as I listen to Trish's message, her words hitting me like a punch to the gut and confirming my own suspicions.

This whole meeting was a diversion to get me out of the way.

I know who Salvadore is!

TRISH

Tony drops me off, refusing my offer of coffee, saying he needs to get back to the station but making sure I get safely back into my apartment before driving away.

I head straight for the living room, not even bothering to remove my coat, my heart hammering as I grab the picture of Prue from its place on the side table.

I gently open the back of the frame, pulling it away and the tiny objects that have been trapped between the frame backing and the photograph drop into my hand, wrapped in tissue paper.

I can hardly believe that they're still here after all these years. The photograph in its frame is one of only two possessions, apart from a few clothes, that Prue and I took with us when we left our old life. Pete knew I would never part with this photograph of our daughter and that if I ever changed the frame I would find what he'd left.

I switch on the laptop, frantically rifling through drawers, knowing I have what I need here somewhere. I finally find what I'm looking for and unwrap the tiny micro SD cards from the tissue paper, sliding one of them into the card adapter.

I plug it into the computer, crossing my fingers that it hasn't been corrupted in any way and sighing in relief when the folder pops up on the desktop. I open it and start clicking on files, smiling as I see they're intact. I scan the files quickly, all of which seem to be documents of some kind, the information in them meaning nothing to me although I'm sure it will prove invaluable to Daryl.

Grabbing a memory stick from the drawer, I copy the files across, repeating the process with the other three micro SD cards without opening any more of the files in my haste to get all the data transferred.

The sudden knock at the door makes me jump, my nerves on edge. I quickly eject the card, wrapping the SD cards in the tissue paper before quickly stashing them back in the picture frame and putting the memory stick in my coat pocket.

I walk to the front door, checking the peephole to see a stranger standing on my doorstep.

"Trish?"

His voice carries through the door and I wonder how he knows my name. "Who wants to know?"

"Trish, my name is Lev. I work with Daryl. He's on his way but he called and asked me to come on ahead and check on you."

I search my memory, trying to recall where I've heard his name before when it suddenly comes to me. I open the door, revealing a tall man with broad shoulders. His head is completely bald, his bright blue eyes warm and friendly as he observes me.

"You're Daryl's handler. Oh!" I clap my hand over my mouth. "I don't think I'm supposed to know that!"

"It's okay. I've been working this case with Daryl so I know he's told you who I am." Lev smiles briefly, his eyes crinkling at the corners. "Like I said, he asked me to come and make sure you're okay. He's been delayed but he received new information about the identity of Salvadore and he thinks you may be in danger after your visit to see Pete. He asked me to come and keep an eye on you until he gets here. Do you mind some company while we wait for him?"

My heart stutters at Lev's words. "Yes of course." I hold the door open and Lev steps inside. I notice the car behind him for the first time, a blond-haired man sitting in the driver's seat.

Lev follows my gaze. "That's my driver," he explains. "He'll wait outside."

I move toward the living room, feeling suddenly chilled despite still wearing my coat and I wrap my arms around myself. "So, Daryl thinks I'm in danger? Why?" I ask, turning to face Lev.

Lev looks at me for a minute before sighing heavily. "May we?" He indicates the sofa.

"Oh! Yes, please sit down." I move to sit in the chair while Lev takes a seat on the sofa.

Lev looks grim. "Daryl called me a half hour ago. He believes he knows who Salvadore is."

"What? But how?" I ask, shocked. "He doesn't even know about the evidence yet." I wonder silently if it has anything to do with the phone message I left for him.

"Peter gave you the evidence?" Lev says, looking at me intently.

"Not exactly, no," I reply,

"Then what?" Lev frowns.

"He told me where it was."

Lev leans back on the sofa, a reluctant smile pulling at his mouth. "Let me guess. It was with you all along."

I nod. "In a place that Pete knew it would be safe. So, how did Daryl work out who Salvadore is?" I ask again.

"One of Salvadore's men came forward saying he was prepared to disclose important information in exchange for protection," Lev explains. "He would only agree to meet with Daryl, which is why he wasn't able to come to the prison with you. However, the man was a no-show and Daryl suspected that the whole thing was a diversion to get him out of the way so that you'd be an easy target if you managed to persuade Pete to disclose the evidence."

My hand flies to my mouth as I process what Lev is telling me. "Who does he think Salvadore is?"

Lev hesitates, his eyes grave. "Tony Cooper. His partner."

My mouth drops open. "Tony? I don't, I mean, I can't..." The thought that Tony, a man Daryl has known half his life, the man I was riding in a car with not a half hour ago, is Salvadore is hard to believe. I close my eyes, already able to imagine the hurt and betrayal Daryl must be feeling.

"Exactly," Lev says, obviously following my train of thought.

"But, I was with him just a little while ago. I even invited him in but he said he had to get back to the station and left. Why would he do that if he thought I could give him the evidence?" I ask, bewildered.

"Because it would be too obvious," Lev says. "He had to be seen leaving, check in at the station, make his presence known. That way no suspicion will fall on him when he makes his way back here, the evidence goes missing and you turn up dead."

I can feel the color drain from my face at Lev's blunt words. It all makes horrible sense. "Tony would have been in a perfect position to know what was going on with the case and Daryl would have been none the wiser," I whisper.

"It's not just Daryl he duped, it's me too. I was supposed to watch Daryl's back and I failed him," Lev sighs angrily, rubbing his hands over his eyes. "But I won't fail him now. I promised him I'd get you out safely along with the evidence and that's exactly what I intend to do. Do you have it?"

I'm no longer listening to Lev, my attention riveted to the hands that he just rubbed over his face, his right hand in particular.

Where the end of his pinkie finger is missing.

Shit! My stomach drops to my feet and my blood turns to ice in my veins as I realize that Lev is lying. *He* is Salvadore. Lev, Daryl's handler, who would also have been in the perfect position to keep up with every development on the case.

What had Guillermo said to Daryl in the alley two days ago?

It's difficult to know who you can trust in your line of work.

In the few seconds it takes me to process all this, I realise that Lev is looking at me expectantly. "I'm sorry, what did you say?" I try to keep my voice steady, not betraying any of the inner turmoil I'm feeling.

"The evidence?" Lev sees my look of confusion. "You have it, right?"

"Sorry, I'm uh, still trying to absorb everything you've told me," I say nervously. "The evidence. Yes of course. I'll, uh, I'll just go and get it."

I start to stand but falter at Lev's next words. "You seem on edge, Trish." He purses his lips, as if deep in thought and then sighs in resignation. "Tell me, what was it that gave me away?"

My heart jumps into my throat. "Um, gave you away?"

"Was it my voice? No? Maybe it was my hair." He smooths his hand over his bald head, grinning wolfishly at his own joke. "Or, maybe it was this." He holds up his right hand, displaying the shorter finger. "You have very expressive eyes, Trish. They give you away. You've just figured out a few things, am I right?"

"I, uh, I don't know what you mean, Lev." I lick my suddenly dry lips, desperately trying to maintain a nonchalant facade while my insides go into meltdown.

Lev ignores me. "Do you want to know how I lost it, Trish? My finger? Let me tell you how it happened." He spreads his arms wide along the back of the sofa, crossing one leg over the other and looking for all the world as if he's merely settling in for a bedtime story.

"I'm sure Daryl told you that I was UC for eight years, working on infiltrating a narcotics operation. What he may not have told you was that I had to do a lot of...questionable things during that time, things that I never, in my worst nightmares, could have imagined." Lev looks at me and the warmth of the smile that greeted me when I answered the door is gone, his blue eyes now devoid of emotion.

89

"Tell me, Trish, do you know what it does to a man every time he has to carry out a vile deed? Something that goes against every moral he's ever learned?" Lev looks at me as if expecting an answer and I shake my head. "I'll tell you. Each time, it kills a little bit of his soul, makes him less than he was before. He's not the same man he was before he snorted that line of coke or jammed that needle in his arm, before he forced another man to overdose on heroin at gunpoint or before he had to cut off the end of his own finger to prove his allegiance to the very criminals he was trying to bring down." Lev's voice is laced with bitterness.

"And you know what I got at the end of it all, Trish? What the force gave me for my hard work and dedication? For the sacrifices I made? Not a fucking thing! A pat on the back and a few sessions with a fucking shrink! As if that could wipe clean all the things I had to do, the things I had to endure. What a fucking travesty for years of dedicated service, about as above and beyond as it gets."

A chill trickles down my back at the things Lev is telling me, along with an unwanted pang of sympathy for the man in front of me. "I'm sorry you had to endure all that, Lev," I whisper.

"I don't need your fucking sympathy, Trish!" Lev spits the words at me, all traces of the charming man now gone, the civilised veneer stripped away as the monster beneath claws his way out.

"You don't deserve any, Lev, not for the things you've done!" Despite my brave words, my heart is throbbing in my throat and fear lends a fine tremor in my muscles.

Lev ignores my outburst. "I want you to imagine what it feels like, Trish, having to saw off your own finger. Shall I get you a knife, and we can find out? I'll even hold your hand down while you do it. Or, perhaps you'd prefer to stick a needle full of heroin in your vein?" He sees the look of terror on my face, "No? Didn't think so."

"Please don't think I'm telling you all this just for the pleasure of frightening you, Trish, because it's so much more than that. I need you to understand that I didn't set out to be the typical good cop gone bad. In fact, I prefer to think of it as bad cop gone good because it seems I'm a far better criminal than I ever was a cop. Don't get me wrong, Trish, I take no pleasure in threatening anyone, least of all a woman, but let me be clear."

Lev sits forward, the smile on his face at complete odds with his cold eyes. "Give me the fucking evidence, or I'll subject you to every single one of the experiences I mentioned earlier. I'm sure you were paying attention, weren't you? You don't have to answer, a simple nod will suffice."

I look at the man in front of me with eyes full of hate, wondering at the chain of events that led him to the choices he's made, the people he's hurt - and not just the people during his time UC, but all those following that, including Prue and myself.

Lev sighs resignedly. "Okay, Trish. I can see I'm going to have to convince you."

For a big man, Lev moves surprisingly quickly, pulling me roughly from the chair and dragging me toward the kitchen. I try to pull away, but he only tightens his hold, his fingers bruising my arms. He turns me roughly so that I'm facing the worktop where Daryl and I were intimate not twenty-four hours ago, a poignant reminder of how much has changed since then.

Lev grabs a handful of my hair and presses his body against my back "Please! Don't!" I choke the words through a throat thick with terror.

"Oh, please, Trish!" I can hear the disgust in Lev's voice as he bends his mouth to my ear. "I'm not about to force myself on you, it's not my style."

"Not your style?" I spit the words at him in stunned disbelief. "Oh, of course not! You just send one of your people to do that kind of messed up shit for you! Diego Martinez, for example." My words are drenched with bitterness.

"That was necessary to keep your ex-husband in line," Lev says, calmly. "I take no pleasure in making those kinds of decisions."

"The kind of decision that makes it okay to rape a thirteen-year-old girl? You could've fooled me!" I choke.

Lev's hold on my hair tightens, bringing tears to my eyes, and the memory of Diego doing the same thing with a knife to my throat almost overwhelms me. "That was a mistake. He was never supposed to touch her that way, just rough her up a little," Lev says, as if that somehow makes everything okay. "Despite what you think, I'm not a complete monster, Trish."

I smother a hysterical laugh at the ridiculous irony of his words as the man who's just claimed he's not a 'complete monster' reaches into the drawer and pulls out a knife, forcing my right hand down against the counter. He subdues my struggles with the weight of his body as he hovers the sharp blade over my pinkie finger. "I thought we'd start out with this." He presses the knife against my skin and I watch in horror as a bead of blood appears, the blade biting into my flesh.

"Stop! Okay, okay. I'll g... give you what you w... want!" I hate the stammer in my voice, the fact that my fear is so evident.

"There now, that wasn't so hard, was it?" Lev lifts the blade away from my finger and places the knife carefully down on the counter next to my hand. "Don't even fucking think about picking up that knife, Trish, or I'll cut every one of your fucking fingers off right before I cut your tongue out of your mouth. Do you understand?"

I nod my head jerkily.

"Good girl." Lev pushes me back toward the living room. "Now, tell me where the evidence is." I can't help the instinctive movement of my eyes to the photograph of Prue on the side table. "Well, shit! There's those expressive eyes giving you away again, Trish."

Those expressive eyes Lev likes to keep referring to are full of hatred as I watch him walk to the table, pick up the photograph and hand it to me. "Open it," he instructs.

I grit my teeth and fumble open the back of the photograph for the second time today, extracting the SD cards wrapped in their protective tissue paper and handing them to Lev.

"And the copy you made, Trish. You're a smart girl, so I know you made a copy."

"I didn't...."

He grabs my chin in one of his hands, his grip bruising as his fingers bite into my face. "Don't fucking lie to me! Shall we go back to the kitchen? Do I really need to prove to you just how inventive I can be with a knife?"

"No," I whisper. "I only had time to make one copy." Hard as it is, I look him in the eye so he can see the truth of my words. "It's in the bedroom."

"Then, by all means, lead the way." Lev swoops a hand in front of him, gesturing toward the bedroom. "No sudden moves, Trish, or you really won't like the consequences."

I walk slowly into the bedroom ahead of Lev until I reach the bed, turning my back to him and bending to open the divan drawer. My coat shifts forward and fear almost chokes me as I risk removing the item I need, concealing it in the folds of material. At the same time, I grasp the memory stick from the pocket with my other hand and turn to Lev, who has now come to stand behind me, holding out the memory stick toward him.

As he reaches for it, my fingers twitch and it clatters it to the floor between us. I step back, terror written all over my face. "I'm sorry, I'm sorry! I... I.. you're making me nervous...!" I lift pleading eyes to Lev.

"Ah, Trish. You don't need to be nervous anymore. Not now you've given me what I want. See how easy that was?" Lev says, bending to retrieve the memory stick from the floor.

In one swift movement, I pull the baseball bat from behind my coat, the second of the only two items we brought with us from our old house, my fingers curling firmly around the solid wood of the handle.

I lift the bat above my head, unleashing an almighty scream of rage as I bring it crashing down against Lev's shaven skull with a satisfying crack, watching blood ooze from the welt on the back of the man's head who sent Diego Martinez to hurt my daughter. He falls to his hands and knees from the force of the blow but doesn't go down, lifting his head to look at me with fury-filled eyes.

"Didn't see that one coming in my expressive eyes, did you, asshole?" I shout at him. "I've had just about all I can take of pieces of shit like you coming into my fucking house, thinking you can threaten me and my family. No more!" I feel the years of anger bubbling to the surface, overwhelming me, consuming me in a blaze of absolute fury.

Lev looks at me, blooding running down the side of his face and neck, his eyes promising me an unholy vengeance. "You have no fucking idea who you're mess..."

I swing the bat again before he can finish, before he has the chance to come at me, smashing it sideways across his face and watching as blood sprays from his mouth onto the floor. This time, he hits the floor, groaning.

"No, Lev. You have no fucking idea who *you're* messing with!" My chest is heaving with exertion and adrenaline as I spit the words at his semi-conscious form.

I stoop down, swiping the memory stick from the floor and sprint for the door, flinging it open and coming to an abrupt halt as I stare down the muzzle of a gun.

DARYL

I hear the sound of a gun discharging as I screech to a halt outside Trish's apartment and fear grips my muscles, almost paralysing me.

I fling the door open and pull my Glock in one movement and my eyes focus on Tony with his gun trained on a man lying in the doorway of Trish's apartment.

Tony glances over at me, acknowledging silently that he's seen me as he moves forward to check the fallen man.

My training takes over as I advance to cover him and relief almost brings me to my knees as I see Trish standing in the doorway, seemingly unharmed, holding a baseball bat. As Tony stoops to secure the other man's weapon, a movement behind Trish catches my eye and I see Lev, gun in hand, staggering toward her, blood running down his face and onto the collar of his shirt.

"Trish! Get down!" I yell.

It takes a split second for Trish to realize what's happening and she drops to the floor as I take the shot. Lev goes down and doesn't move.

I watch as Trish tries to stand, but her legs won't support her and she slides down the wall in a dead faint.

Backup arrives, along with two EMT units who get straight to work on the two men, both of whom are still alive. The temptation to put a bullet through Lev's head and be done with it is almost overwhelming but Trish is my priority right now.

Tony and I lift her and carry her into the living room, laying her gently on the sofa. I sit next to her, pulling a cushion underneath her head for support and checking her pulse.

Tony leaves me alone with Trish while he goes outside to brief the officers on the scene. I check her over for wounds, sighing with relief when I find nothing other than blood on the pinkie finger of her right hand and the beginnings of some bruising around her jaw. That doesn't mean she doesn't have internal injuries though and my blood runs cold as I think about what she must have endured in the time it took us to get here.

As soon as I received Trish's message I knew exactly who Salvadore was and
wasted no time calling Tony to haul ass over here. He'd just arrived back at the station but had headed straight back to Trish's apartment once I'd told him the situation. I broke every speed limit to get here, my fear for Trish overriding all else.

Trish groans, pulling me from my thoughts, as her eyelids flicker and open. Her eyes round in terror as she remembers where she is and what's happened and she tries to sit up. "Salvadore! Lev is Salvadore! He's here!"

"Shhh. It's okay, Trish. It's all over now. We got him. You're safe." I gently push her back down on the sofa, stroking her dishevelled hair back from her face. She looks pale and shaken and absolutely beautiful as my eyes greedily take her in.

Trish groans, flinging an arm over her eyes. "I can't believe I passed out! I was being such a badass and then I went and ruined it all!"

"Are you kidding me? You've just been through an ordeal, you could've died! You are the most badass woman I've ever known!" I smile with relief, pulling her uninjured hand to my mouth and kissing her fingers. "Remind me to never piss you off, especially when you're holding a baseball bat."

Trish grins. "I was pretty awesome, wasn't I?" Her grin fades as quickly as it appeared and she bursts into tears, shock settling in as she buries her face in her hands and sobs.

I pull her into my arms, holding her to me tightly, trying to draw her into me as the terror I experienced during the last hour washes over me.

Trish pulls back to look at me, her eyes wet from her tears. "You're shaking!"

"Jesus, Trish. I was so fucking scared. I thought I'd lost you! When I got here and saw you were okay, the relief nearly brought me to my knees. Then Lev came at you from behind and everything seemed to slow down. I knew in that split second that if I missed, if Lev got to you, my life would be over too." The thought of being in this world without Trish now is unbearable.

Trish pulls my head toward her, her lips finding mine in what feels like a meeting of souls rather than a mere kiss. "I'm okay, baby. As long as I'm with you, I'll always be okay. More than okay. Fucking awesome." Her smile is back as I wipe the tears from her eyes with my thumbs. She reaches into the pocket of her coat and pulls out a memory stick. "Lev has the original SD cards but I took copies."

"You are amazing, you know that?" I grin at her.

Trish raises her eyebrows suggestively. "You can show me how amazing you think I am later."

Before I can reply, we're interrupted by the paramedics who've come to check Trish over. I move out of the way, allowing them to do their job and ten minutes later they declare Trish unharmed apart from her finger, which has been cleaned and dressed, and some minor bruising.

Tony appears in front of me. "They've taken Lev and the other guy to the hospital. They should both pull through but they won't be bothering anyone for a long time. You need to..."

I hold up a hand, interrupting Tony, knowing what he's going to say. "Trish isn't giving a statement today, Tony. She needs to get out of here so I'm taking her to my place. The paperwork can wait until tomorrow."

"Hey, you won't get any arguments from me," Tony holds both his hands up in surrender. "I was just gonna say, you need to get yourselves out of here. I'll deal with it. After all, what's another shitload of paperwork on top of the shitload I've already got," he grins.

"Thanks, Tony. For everything. I appreciate it," I say, trying to convey the depth of my gratitude.

"You'd do the same for me, D," Tony replies. "Although, I must admit, you do like to keep things interesting!" He laughs, slapping me on the shoulder before making his way back outside.

I go back to Trish, holding out my hand and pulling her to her feet. "Come on, honey. We're getting out of here."

A look of relief crosses her face and I know I was right in wanting to get her away from here after the trauma of recent events. "Where are we going?" she asks.

"Back to mine."

Trish hesitates. "I need clothes…"

"This is a crime scene now, Trish. I'll come back tomorrow for whatever you need."

She nods wearily, making no further objections as I lead her out toward the front door. She blanches as she sees the blood on the floor from both Lev and Andy and I quickly usher her to the car, opening the door and buckling her in.

"How did you figure it out?" Trish asks once we're on the road and heading toward my apartment. "That Lev was Salvadore?"

"I was suspicious when the informant didn't show, and then I started putting things together, remembering what Guillermo said in the alley." I tell Trish how her phone message had confirmed all my suspicions. "Thank God, I picked up your message when I did! Any later and …" I can't even contemplate what would have happened.

Trish reaches across and puts her hand on my thigh, squeezing gently. "I'm fine," she reassures me.

I reach down, grabbing her hand and bringing it to my mouth. "I can't believe how well you're holding up after everything you've been through," I say. "I can't stop imagining what Lev could have done to you!"

"Oh, he threatened me," she says, holding up her injured finger. "Said he was going to start with my finger and then pump me full of heroin if I didn't give him what he wanted." She shivers and I squeeze the steering wheel until my knuckles turn white. "But, scared as I was, I just kept holding on to the thought that I would never let him make a victim of me. No one will, not ever again," she says, vehemently. "There was something very freeing and satisfying about smashing the shit out of him with the same baseball bat that Prue used on Diego Martinez."

I glance across at her, a reluctant smile pulling at my mouth. "Divine retribution?"

She gives me a weary smile. "There's nothing divine about my kind of retribution."

Twenty minutes later I pull up outside my apartment, walking round to open Trish's door and help her out. Not that she needs my help but it feels good nonetheless.

Trish follows me through the entrance hall into the main living area. "Wow, nice place," she says, looking around and taking everything in. "I could fit my apartment in here three times over."

I shrug. "It's four walls. It could do with a woman's touch," I suggest, raising my eyebrows at her.

She walks toward me and I open my arms, wrapping her up and loving the way she fits against me. She sighs against my chest, a sound of pure contentment and my heart swells.

101

"Which woman did you have in mind?" she teases, lifting her face to look up at me.

"Well, there was this blond interior designer I met once...ow!" I mock grimace, rubbing my arm where she's just punched me before bending to her mouth and stealing a kiss. "There's only one woman for me," I murmur against her lips, "and she's standing right here in my arms, where she should be."

"I'm not sure she'll be standing for much longer," Trish says, wearily. "I'm exhausted."

"It's the shock. You need something to eat, a hot shower and bed. In that order," I say. "Come on. Sit down and I'll make us a sandwich."

Trish takes a seat on a stool at the breakfast bar, her eyes following me as I move around the kitchen gathering the ingredients for chicken salad sandwiches. "I could get used to this," she says as she watches me rinse the lettuce. "Feels very domesticated."

"After what happened today, I think we could both do with a little normalcy," I say, giving her a wry smile.

We sit down to eat our sandwiches in comfortable silence and once we're done, I clear away our plates and pull Trish to her feet, leading through the bedroom and into the bathroom.

I turn on the shower and turn to her, slowly stripping her out of her clothes. She lifts her arms as I tug her sweater over her head, unbuttoning her pants and sliding them down her legs. I take a minute to enjoy the sight of her standing before me in her bra and panties, before divesting her of those too, leaving her completely naked in front of me. She stands there, her body completely open to my eyes, all creamy white skin and beautiful curves, her nipples hardening under my hot gaze.

I begin to strip off my own clothes, watching as Trish's eyes trail down my body from my broad shoulders and chest down to my abs, lingering on my swollen cock, and it's all I can do to stop myself from laying her on the floor and burying myself in her moist heat. I clamp down on my needs, knowing we have plenty of time - time I didn't think we would have a few hours ago. Right now, I need to take care of her.

I pull her under the spray of the shower and the hot water washes over us, helping to eliminate some of the stress of the day, much like it did two days ago. Those two days feel like an eternity with everything that's happened not least of which is Trish escaping death not once, but twice.

I squeeze some shower gel into my hands, lathering it before sweeping my hands over Trish's body, gently massaging her supple skin through the suds until she moans in pleasure.

"You have magic hands," she says, turning to face me and looping her arms around my neck, bringing my head down to hers for a scorching kiss. Our tongues tangle together as the kiss becomes heated and my blood catches fire.

"You need sleep," I gasp against her mouth, trying to quell the demands of my body, knowing how tired she is.

"I need you more!" she moans, sweeping her hands around my hips to my engorged cock, making me jerk involuntarily at the sweetness of her touch.

"Fuck!" I groan, my control slipping as her slick fingers move back and forth on me, her hands working my stiff shaft.

She trails kisses from my mouth, along my jaw to my ear, biting my earlobe. "Make love to me, Daryl. I want you to fuck me hard and deep until I can't see or feel anything but you. Help me forget today."

I know what she needs because it's what I need too. To feel her under me, over me, to lose myself in her and have her lose herself in me so that we can escape the realities of the day, if only for a short while.

I crush her to me, grabbing one thigh and lifting her leg so that my needy cock is pressed against her pussy as I kiss her deeply, groaning as my need to get inside her becomes overwhelming.

I turn off the shower, not even bothering to dry off as I grab a large towel and spread it on the floor so that she can lie down on it. I press her legs open and kneel between her thighs, pulling her hips toward me so that her ass is resting on my knees. Her sweet pussy is bared to me as I slide my fingers between her juicy folds, opening her up as I position myself and slide my length inside her in one smooth motion.

"Oh, God!" I groan at the sensation of her tight channel enveloping me, gritting my teeth to stop myself from immediately emptying my load into her. I've never experienced anything like the physical and emotional connection I feel with this woman, the strength and depth of it staggers me.

An urgency takes root in me as I withdraw my cock, looking down to see it glistening with her juices, the sight turning me on like nothing else as I thrust inside her wet channel again. Trish cries out, lifting her hips even closer so that my next thrust sinks even further into her tight depths.

"Let me see you touch yourself, baby,' I growl, as I thrust into her again.

A blush stains her cheeks as she looks at me. "I can't... I mean, in front of you?" she asks, embarrassed.

"Right now. I want to see you touch yourself like you did when you came for me on the phone," I demand, the caveman in me surging forth. "I want to see you stroke that plump clit and those hard nipples. Show me," I demand.

She moans at my words and I hold her hips as I pull back and surge into her again. Trish arches her back, her perfect tits jutting upward, her nipples hard crests of desire.

She reaches down, running her hands over her tits, playing with her nipples before sliding her hands down her body, slipping a finger into her wet slit and moaning loudly as she rubs herself.

The sight is so fucking hot I feel like my cock is going to implode and I increase the tempo of my hips, watching Trish's fingers buried in her pussy and coated with her juices as she works them against her hard nub.

"That's right, honey. Keep working it with your fingers. Can you feel it building?" I gasp. "I can feel your pussy tightening around me, squeezing my cock so hard, Trish! It feels unbelievable!"

She thrashes her head from side to side below me as the rhythm of my hips and the friction of her finger sends her hurtling over the edge.

"Oh, God! Oh, God! Oh, God!" she cries out, as she grinds herself against me, her climax arching her back up off the floor. The sight of her cumming sends me crashing into my own orgasm with one last pump of my hips, the pleasure almost unbearable as I empty my hot cum inside her, filling her up.

I collapse on top of her, trying to hold my weight on my elbows so I don't crush her, my breathing ragged as the fine tremors of pleasure from my ball busting climax slowly fade.

Trish pushes her fingers through my hair as she pulls me down for her soft kiss. "I love you," she whispers, her lips clinging to mine. "So much!"

"I love you too, honey. More than I ever thought possible."

When I feel my legs can support me again, I stand and pull Trish to her feet and we climb into bed. Trish burrows into me so that our bodies are pressed together as I pull the covers over us.

"I'm not sure I deserve to be this happy," she chokes and I look down to see tears streaming down her cheeks. "I never thought I would find someone like you."

I tip her chin up so she's looking at me. "You deserve to be happy more than anyone," I reassure her softly. "Especially after everything you've been through, everything you've survived. You never let it break your spirit or stop your kindness toward others. It's one of the first things I noticed about you when I started coming to the diner, the warmth you share with people, and it's one of the many reasons I fell in love with you."

Trish's face crumples at my words as the tears flow freely and I hold her even tighter. "It's okay, I've got you," I murmur, smoothing her hair back from her face. "Just let it all out." My heart aches as she cries, even though I know her tears are a much-needed form of release.

Eventually her sobs quiet and she pulls back to look at me with eyes that are red and swollen, reaching up to cup my face. "Do you ever wonder what your life would have been like if you'd just taken a left instead of a right?"

I think for a minute before answering. "Making decisions, knowing what I want, has always come easily to me. My life was mapped out from the moment I lost my parents. I never questioned my decisions until I met you. I kept telling myself that I couldn't get emotionally involved with you but my heart had other plans." A wry smile tugs at my mouth. "So, I guess if there's one thing I could do differently, it would be to have never put you at risk like that. From the moment I met you, for the first time ever, my mind wasn't on the job and it put us both in danger."

I turn my face to kiss her palm as she strokes my cheek. "But you know what? Sometimes the wrong decisions bring us to the right places and, for me, that place is you. And now I've found you, I realise how empty my life was without you."

Trish pulls me to her and kisses me softly. "One of the hardest decisions I ever had to make was whether to walk away from my marriage or try harder. I chose to stay and try harder, for Prue's sake. That's the decision I'll have to live with for the rest of my life," she sighs.

I raise an eyebrow. "So, what you're saying is that you should have been able to predict the future? No one can do that. A decision is just a decision - it's only the outcome that makes it a good or bad one. None of us has the ability to know which way it will go at the time. How can you put that kind of expectation on yourself when you would never put it on someone else?"

Trish's face becomes thoughtful and I can see that my words have struck a chord. "I never really thought about it like that before." A glimmer of a smile touches her mouth. "Are you sure it's not you that's studying for a counselling degree?"

"Well, I don't like to brag, honey, but feel free to call me Dr Freud anytime you like," I grin.

Trish smiles and it lights up her whole face. It's a sight I hope I get to spend the next forty-odd years enjoying.

"Thank you, honey," she says, and my heart melts just a little more at her endearment. "You've breathed new life into me.

Made me realize that I am worthy of being loved. The amazing sex is just frosting," she teases.

"Frosting?" I smirk. "Now there's an idea! Which parts of you would you like me to frost?"

"Behave!" She slaps me lightly, laughing. "And, all over," she giggles, answering my question anyway.

I file that one away as Trish snuggles into me again and we both finally give in to our exhaustion.

EPILOGUE
Three Months Later
TRISH

"Surprise!"

My mouth falls open as I walk out of the diner bathroom to see all my friends standing there.

In the few minutes I've been in the restroom, the place has been transformed into a kaleidoscope of colour, with multi-colored balloons, streamers, and banners that read, 'Good Luck'. A huge cake sits on one of the tables with the words 'We'll Miss You' piped in pink frosting.

I can feel the prick of tears behind my eyes as I look around at my friends, hardly able to believe that this is all for me. "I only went to pee!" I laugh through my tears.

Barb bustles forward, enveloping me in a warm hug, her own eyes glossy with emotion. "You didn't think you were going to finish your last shift here without a bit of a send-off, did you, honey?"

I scan the room, seeing a smiling Helene and Rosie, who also work at the diner, along with several customers I've served over the years who've become friends. "I can't believe you did this!" I exclaim.

"Nothing less than you deserve after so many years of coffee refills," Barb chuckles. "Come and sit." She directs me to the booth where the cake is sitting on the table. "You're now officially a customer too," she says, wiping a tear from her eye before turning to the rest of my friends. "I know we all wish Trish the very best on her new path. Life is all about new beginnings and our friend is getting two – one as a fully qualified counsellor with a new job and the other with the tall hunk of manhood that is Daryl Jacobs!"

Laughter echoes around the diner and my heart hurts a little at the thought of leaving this place, even though I know it's the right time for me to go. I have so many fond memories here along with the friendships I've formed over the years.

"So, let's all raise our coffee cups in a toast to an amazing lady and someone I'm honoured to call my friend." Barb looks at me. "To Trish!"

"To Trish!"

I grab a napkin and dab at the tears on my cheeks as everyone toasts me. "Thank you so much! This means the world to me and I'm going to miss you all but I want to say a special thanks to Barb." I turn to face my friend. "You helped me when I was desperately in need, took my daughter and I into your home and gave me the opportunity to get back on my feet again. I can never thank you enough. I love you."

Barb has tears running down her cheeks as she hugs me again. "Why do you always make me cry?" she sniffs. "I love you too. And I'll always be here for you." She pulls away, all practicality again as she says, "Right then, who wants cake?"

Two hours later, we're all chock full of cake and coffee. I sit back in my seat, groaning and holding my stomach. "That cake was divine but I'm going to need to stop eating for three days to burn it all up!

"I'm sure there are better ways you can burn off those calories," Helena, who's sitting opposite me, says with a wink. "If I had a man like Daryl, I'm pretty sure I'd be burning calories day and night!"

"Like you need to!" I grin at the pretty brunette. Helena started working at the diner about five years ago but we don't often get to see each other as she's always worked opposite shifts to me.

"So, any plans to make things more permanent?" Helena asks. "With you and Daryl, I mean?"

I shrug, pretending a carelessness I don't really feel. "There's no hurry. I know how he feels about me and it's enough that we're living together."

I haven't been back to my apartment since everything that happened there with Lev and Daryl and I have been living together at his apartment. We've settled into life together as if we've always been together and I've never been happier.

Daryl hasn't mentioned marriage since the night before my visit to the prison and even though I never expected to want that kind of commitment ever again, meeting Daryl changed all that.

I know he loves me but I can't help thinking that maybe he's changed his mind about the whole getting married part. I haven't wanted to broach subject because he's been pulling such long hours to prepare everything for Lev's imminent trial. Today is the day that everything is finalised and it'll be a huge relief to both of us.

I'm pulled from my reverie by the sound of the door opening behind me.

"Talk of the devil," Helena says, grinning at me knowingly.

I turn, surprised to see Daryl walking in as I wasn't expecting to see him until later. As always, he takes my breath away, all broad shoulders and icy blue eyes. Even his dark hair is sexily tousled and my hands itch with the urge to run my fingers through it. Today, there's an intensity in his blue eyes as he approaches the table and stops in front of me.

I look up at him, about to say hi, when he drops to one knee in front of me. My eyes widen as I try to register what I'm seeing, watching as he produces a small box from his pocket, a hush settling over the diner as my friends realize what's about to happen.

Daryl clears his throat and my heart swells, knowing that he's completely out of his comfort zone right now. "I'm not a man of fancy words but it seemed only right to do this here. This is where we first met, where I had the pleasure of getting to know the amazing woman that you are. You've become the reason I get out of bed every morning and my last thought every night. I love you. It's as simple as that."

Daryl opens the box to reveal a beautiful silver solitaire diamond ring. "Trish Daniels, will you marry me?"

I slide along the seat and kneel on the floor in front of him. "Yes, I'll marry you Daryl Jacobs!" I launch myself at him and his arms envelop me as he kisses me soundly to the whoops and cheers of everyone around us.

I pull back, an insane grin on my face as I gaze into the eyes of the man I love so deeply and completely that I feel as if I may burst with it. Daryl grins back at me and leans in for another kiss before pulling me to my feet and slipping the ring on my finger, kissing my knuckle where it rests snugly.

In the next instant, I'm squealing in a very un-ladylike manner as he sweeps me off my feet and into his arms. "What are you doing? You'll give yourself a hernia!" I shriek, then giggle like a schoolgirl as cheers erupt around us.

Daryl turns to face everyone. "If you'll excuse me, I'm taking my fiancé home so that I can ravish her."

"Richard Gere, eat your heart out!" Barb calls after us as Daryl strides to the door and I blow her a kiss and wave at my friends as we leave.

Daryl sets me on my feet by the passenger door of the car, which is parked just outside, but doesn't release me, his hands holding my hips and pressing me against him so that I can feel the evidence of his arousal. His head dips to mine and he kisses me deeply until I'm moaning, needing him naked so I can do all the things I want to do to him.

"Let's go home," I murmur against his mouth.

Daryl groans and rests his forehead against mine before releasing me reluctantly and crossing to the driver's side.

Once we're both buckled in and on our way home, Daryl reaches for my hand, enveloping it in his and my heart skips as I catch sight of my shiny engagement ring, not yet accustomed to the sight of it on my finger. Pete and I never had the money for an engagement ring, so wearing Daryl's ring feels extra special.

"It's done." Daryl glances across at me and I can see the relief on his face.

"Thank God!" I breathe, knowing he's referring to the case against Lev.

"We've got prints from their weapons and from the knife that Lev used on you. The evidence from Pete, along with your statement means the case is as watertight as it gets," Daryl says.

"That's great news, honey," I squeeze his hand a little tighter.

"One surprising piece of information did crop up while we were finalising our investigations," Daryl says. "Lev has a daughter."

I lift shocked eyes to his.

"I know," Daryl says, at my shocked look. "I feel sorry for the kid. She's barely twenty-years-old and has no idea who her real father is and from what I can tell, Lev doesn't know of her existence either. It seems her real mother took off when she found out she was pregnant and died under suspicious circumstances six months after she gave birth. The only reason we found out that Lev had fathered a child was because she put his name on the birth certificate, an odd thing to do considering she ran away from him. The baby was adopted by an older couple who couldn't have kids of their own and who now live, would you believe, in Bakersfield," Daryl says, casting me a sideways glance.

"You're kidding!" I burst out, hardly able to believe that Lev is a father, let alone that his daughter lives in the same place as Prue. "Talk about coincidence! Maybe Prue knows her?"

"I don't like coincidences, they make me feel uncomfortable," Daryl says uneasily. "And it's highly unlikely that she and Prue would have crossed paths, seeing as Bakersfield has a population of almost four hundred thousand people."

"Yeah, I guess you're right," I say, still wrapping my head round the fact that Lev has a child. A chilling thought suddenly occurs to me. "Is she in any kind of danger?"

"Not so long as her identity remains a secret. I'm sure Lev has enemies that wouldn't hesitate to use his daughter against him, if the truth came out," Daryl says, ominously.

I sigh sadly, thinking of the girl who's only a few years younger than my Prue and hoping that she remains blissfully ignorant of her real father's identity. Thankfully, now that Lev is headed for a long spell, the chances of her ever meeting him are slim to none.

Once Lev had sufficiently recovered from his wounds, he was transferred to Stanislaus correctional facility with no chance of bail, pending trial. It's been a stressful time, especially for Daryl who's been working every hour under the sun, making sure there are no loopholes, that every procedure is followed and every measure taken to ensure a guilty verdict, not only for Lev but everyone else involved in his operation.

The long hours have taken their toll and I've often been asleep when he's crawled into bed in the early hours, stirring only to snuggle against him and waking the next morning to find him already gone. I knew Daryl needed to see this through to the bitter end, for my sake and for his peace of mind, and I've given him my full support despite us having to sacrifice so much of our time together of late.

"I'm so proud of you," I say, squeezing Daryl's hand. "You gave up so much to bring Lev and his operation down. I'm just sorry it turned out to be someone you thought you could trust."

"Me too. I can't believe I missed all the signs," he says, his voice filled with self-disgust. "I could have lost you!" He clears his throat and I can feel the emotion rolling off him, knowing how much he's struggled with the guilt of not figuring out the truth about Lev until it was almost too late.

"You're looking at an expert when it comes to guilt and self-condemnation," I say. "I tortured myself for years wondering why I missed all the signs with Pete, but it's easy to miss signs we aren't looking for in the first place. The truth is, sometimes the closer we are to someone the less we're able to see the bigger picture. It's taken a long time but I've finally realized that I'm not responsible for another person's deceit, no more than you are."

Daryl looks at me with eyes full of love. "You are going to make a fantastic counsellor."

"I have Barb to thank for that too," I smile, thinking of my friend. Barb's late husband was the headteacher at a local school before he died and Barb has stayed in touch with many of the faculty there. She gave me the heads up when she heard the current school counsellor was approaching retirement and wanted to reduce her hours.

I'd gone for the interview, never imagining I'd get the job but the panel had liked me instantly and, for once, my age and previous life experiences have stood me in good stead.

The job is two and a half days a week but I have the benefit of being mentored by the existing counsellor, a lovely lady called Susan, whom I met at the interview and is a veritable fountain of information and support.

My musings are interrupted as we pull up outside the apartment. Daryl cuts the engine and before he can move I shimmy over until I'm straddling him in the driver's seat. "I have cake I need to work off," I whisper, raising my eyebrows and pressing myself against the growing hardness of his crotch.

"How much cake?" Daryl growls, pushing his hands through my hair and pulling my mouth toward his.

"Three slices," I murmur, nibbling his bottom lip. "Three *big* slices."

"And how long do you think it will take to work that off?"

"Three days, at least," I moan, as he runs his tongue along my lips.

"Well, it's a good job it's the weekend," he breathes, his hands moving from my hair to cup my breasts, his thumbs finding my nipples through my uniform.

I arch my back, pressing against his hands and grinding against his hardness as heat floods through my bloodstream.

"It's been too long!" I gasp, loving the feel of his hands on me. "I want you so badly!"

"I know, honey, and I'm sorry I've been so distant," Daryl apologises. "I needed to make sure that bastard could never hurt you again! When I think of what could've happened…"

I place my fingers against his lips. "Shhh. You have nothing to apologise for. I understand. I know if it was you I'd do everything in my power to keep you safe." I lean into him, teasing his mouth with mine. "But I have missed you. I've missed this," I breathe, nibbling at his lips until he groans, his hands grabbing my thighs and grinding me against him.

"I need to get you inside and strip you naked before I cum in my boxers," Daryl moans, his mouth seeking a deeper contact with mine as I toy with his lips.

No sooner are we through the front door than Daryl pulls me into his arms, his mouth on mine as he backs me up toward the living area.

Our hands are frenzied as we release buttons and zips, tugging the clothes from each other's bodies until we're both naked, our bodies moulded together as we kiss deeply.

I moan, pushing my fingers through his hair as his mouth leaves a fiery trail down my jaw to my neck, nibbling and biting at the sensitive skin.

I nudge him so he backs up, pushing on his shoulders so that he sits on the sofa behind him before straddling him. My hands reach for his swollen cock and I slide the end of him against my already wet folds, coating him in my juices. I position the tip of his shaft against my opening, so ready for him that I'm able to sink down on him in one smooth motion.

Daryl's hips jerk under me at the exquisite contact and my head rolls back at the feeling of him inside me again after weeks of abstinence. "I love you so much!" I moan as I begin to ride him, finding the right position so that my clit is stimulated with each movement against him.

"I love you too, baby!" he groans, thrusting his hips up as I sink down on his length. He cups my breasts, his mouth finding the hard peaks of my nipples as he tongues them, the sensation shooting straight to my core so that I can feel my orgasm building deep within my womb.

"I love fucking you like this!" I gasp, holding his head against me as our movements become more urgent. "Hard and fast and so deep!"

"Dear God, Trish. You're gonna be the death of me!" Daryl grunts as he pounds into me, our bodies coming together with a forcefulness that should be painful but which only serves to heighten the pleasure.

He bites my nipple and the small sting of pain makes me cry out in pleasure as I hover on the edge of my climax. "I'm gonna cum!" I gasp.

Daryl stills his hips, breathing harshly as his hands grip my thighs, stopping my movements. "Not yet, honey. Just stop for a minute, let it back away and then we're going to start again. I want you to have the best fucking orgasm you've ever had!"

I press my forehead against his, willing my breathing to slow as my body calms a little. Daryl is also struggling to control his reactions and I kiss him softly, my tongue tangling with his as we slowly begin to move against each other again, feeling the fires burn quicker and hotter than before.

In mere seconds, I'm moaning, teetering on the edge again and Daryl stills our movements once more until I'm moaning and shivering on top of him.

"This time, honey. I'm going to fill you so deep and hard and we're gonna fly over the edge together. I wanna feel that sweet pussy gripping me tight as we cum!" he demands.

His thumbs tease my nipples and I look down, the sight of his cock moving in and out of me beyond hot as I hover on the cusp of my orgasm for the third time.

I feel the spasms bite into me, my internal muscles quivering as my release overwhelms me and I throw my head back, screaming with the force of my orgasm. I'm barely aware of Daryl's own hoarse shout as he rivets himself against me, emptying his hot cum into my body as I continue to squeeze my internal muscles on him, pulling every last drop of his essence into me.

I collapse against him, catching my breath after our intense lovemaking, my hands stroking his hair, his face, every part of him I can reach.

Daryl nuzzles his face into my neck, his teeth nipping at my skin as we just hold each other, revelling in the feeling of closeness following such mind-blowing pleasure.

Eventually, we head to the bathroom, showering together as we rekindle the intimacy that has been missing from our relationship with the demands of the last few weeks. Our hands linger as we bathe each other, the need for words redundant for now as we express our love for each other through gentle touches and soft kisses.

After we're done, I wrap myself in a robe while Daryl pulls on a pair of shorts and t-shirt and we sit down to eat in companionable silence until I suddenly remember something.

"Oh! I need to ring Prue! Tell her the good news," I grin, holding up my left hand and waggling my finger.

Prue came for a visit about a month ago to celebrate her twenty-third birthday and she and Daryl hit it off immediately. By the time she left to go back to Bakersfield a few days later, it was as if they'd known each other forever. It helps that she can see how happy I am, how much Daryl and I love each other.

Daryl and I had agreed not to tell Prue anything about the events with Lev or my visit to see Pete. I feel guilty, having never kept secrets from her before but I know that it's for her own safety and peace of mind. As a mother, it's the least I can do for my daughter after all the pain she's suffered in her young life.

"Go ring our girl, honey," Daryl smiles at me across the table.

Prue picks up at the first ring. "Hi, Mom."

"Hey, sweet girl. How are you?"

"I'm good. You?" she asks.

"I'm good. Great, actually," I say, unable to keep the excitement out of my voice. "Daryl asked me to marry him and I said yes!"

"Oh, Mom! That's wonderful news! Congratulations to you both! Tell Daryl he's achieved the impossible!" Prue chuckles.

"I'll tell him," I laugh. "I never thought in a million years I'd get married again after your father."

"Well, you know what they say - true love conquers all!"

"It certainly does, honey. Talking of," my voice takes on a teasing note, "any love life updates you want to share with your Mom?"

"Mom, seriously!" Prue's voice takes on an edge of exasperation. "I am so not having this conversation with you again."

"I worry about you, Prue. It's not good to be on your own," I say, a twinge of guilt rearing its ugly head.

"I know, Mom, but it's not that simple. I'd rather be on my own than end up like you and dad," Prue says, before adding quickly, "sorry, Mom. I didn't mean it like that."

"Yes, you did, honey. And you don't need to apologize for speaking the truth, Prue."

"Anyway, it's not like I haven't tried. I've dated – even signed up to one of those online dating sites but it's just not for me," Prue sighs.

"Prue, you are an amazing, funny, caring person and any man would be lucky to have you," I say firmly. "I'm your mother so I should know. You are a beautiful woman, curves and all. Get out there and show them what they're missing. I know what happened was awful but don't let that experience stop you from living your life. If you do, he's won." Words I'm only just heeding myself.

"I know you're right, Mom," Prue sighs. "It's just that some things aren't that easy to forget."

"We both know that, honey. I only wish I'd gotten us out sooner, that it hadn't taken that man putting his hands on you to make me realize how bad things really were."

"It wasn't your fault, Mom. None of us knew what Dad had gotten himself into. You did everything you could to make it work, even when it meant sacrificing your own happiness," Prue says, repeating the words she's said to me many times before.

"I know that now," I murmur. "It's hard to see the nightmare you're living in when you don't know any different. It's like lying in the sun for too long and not realizing that you've burned your skin until it's too late, only I didn't realize it wasn't just me getting burned. You were too. He was a good man before it all went to hell. I almost left it too late."

I swallow back tears, refusing to let memories of the past overwhelm me anymore. I'm finally moving on with my life. With Daryl. "But, I've finally forgiven myself, Prue. I know now that I can't move on until I do. Daryl and I haven't known each other long, but he and I are just … right together. More so than it ever was with your father. If someone like him can love me just as I am, truly love me, then I have to believe I'm worthy of that love."

"I'm so happy to hear you say that, Mom. You deserve to be happy." Prue's voice is full of emotion.

"And what about you, Prue? What about what you deserve?" I ask, softly.

"I'm still figuring that out, Mom."

I finish my call with Prue a few minutes later, staring at the blank screen of my cell phone as I mull over Prue's words, some of my happiness eclipsed by the sadness I can still hear in my daughter's voice as I wonder if my girl will ever be free of her own demons.

Strong arms come around me from behind and I lean back against Daryl, his closeness comforting me, as always.

"Everything okay, honey?" he asks.

"Yeah. I just worry about her, you know?" I sigh, turning to face him and resting my head against his chest.

"I know. And we can share that worry together now but she needs to walk her own path, find her own peace with everything. We'll be there for her if she needs us," Daryl reassures me, and my heart swells at his words, knowing how much he means them.

"I know she doesn't *need* a man to complete her but I wish she could find someone that she can have fun with and who makes her realize that she's not defined by her past, just like you have for me." I lift my head to look at him, losing myself in his blue eyes. "You loved me even when I couldn't love myself."

"And you showed me what love really is," Daryl replies, bending to kiss me. "Let's not worry about tomorrow, or next week," he murmurs against my mouth, his hands smoothing up and down my back through my robe. "We've been doing that for the last three months. Let's just enjoy the here and now, that you've agreed to be my wife. And that you still have two and a half pieces of cake to work off," he grins.

"Earlier was only worth half a piece?" I say, in mock horror.

"Barely a half," Daryl confirms, grabbing my ass and pulling me against his blatant hard-on.

"Think we can burn off a whole piece this time?" I ask, huskily, sweeping my hands up underneath his t-shirt and stroking his nipples with my thumbs.

"Let's go find out!" Daryl growls, sweeping me up into his arms for the second time today and heading for the bedroom.

A long time later, breathing hard and utterly spent, we both agree that those three pieces of cake are history.

Keep reading for an excerpt from Playing Hard, Prue and Jake's story and Book 2 of the Play Series

PRUE

The party is already in full swing as I climb out of the cab and music blares from the open door and windows as people mill around out front, drinking beer and goofing around.

For the hundredth time, I tug on the neckline of the dress, trying to adjust it to cover a little more of my generous boobs where it dips into a deep V at the front. It's revealing more of my rounded flesh than I'm comfortable with but the white dress, blonde wig and bright red lipstick are all part of my costume tonight.

I'm not even sure why I'm here - it's not like I even know Carolyn that well. We met at the self-defence class we both attend and got talking and next thing I knew I'd accepted her invite to her fancy-dress birthday party. At the time, it had sounded like a great idea as my lack of finances mean I don't often get to go out and have a little fun, but now I'm just wanting to head home to my bed which is calling me after a long day at work.

I decide I'll stay just long enough to have a drink and show my face.

I make my way past Spiderman who's shooting "webs" at his

friends from devices strapped to his wrists and as I approach the front door I notice Supergirl, obviously not feeling so super, as she vomits all over the flower beds.

Classy.

I push my way through the throng of people lining the hallway and into the carnage that is Carolyn's birthday party.

The living area is packed with people dancing and drinking and couples making out in dark corners. The pervasive smell of sweat and pot is heavy in the air. My nose wrinkles in distaste, having more reason than most to hate those smells. A keg of beer sits on a stand next to the kitchen hatch and a group of guys dressed as ninja turtles are gathered around it downing shots.

"Prue, you came!"

I hear a familiar squeal behind me and turn to see Carolyn. She's a complete Disney nerd, so I'm not at all surprised to see her dressed as Tinkerbell, complete with gossamer wings and wand. "Hey, Carolyn. Sorry I'm late, I came straight from work. Happy birthday!"

"Thanks, Prue." Carolyn shoves a plastic cup of punch under my nose. "Here ya go! You got some catching up to do."

I'm pretty sure Carolyn is already buzzed, judging by the way she's swaying on her feet and slurring her words. "Your get-up looks amazeballs by the way. You look hot as Marilyn Monroe, I almost didn't recognize you with the blonde wig!"

I take the cup from her and hold it up to my nose before taking a sip. The liquid burns a fiery trail down my throat and makes my eyes water. "There's a lot of people here," I cough, indicating the packed room around us.

"Yeah, my brother crashed the party with some of his friends,"

Carolyn replies, pointing at the ninja turtles by the beer keg who now appear to be trying to out-ninja each other. Or dancing – it's hard to tell.

"Hey, Carolyn!" Elvis appears behind her in a white jewelled one-piece slit to the waist with fake chest hair, "Maisie needs you – she's hurling up on the flower beds out front. I've been holding her hair up for the last five minutes but I think she may need to go home."

"Wunnerful!" Carolyn wobbles on her feet and sloshes some of her drink down the front of her outfit. "Mingle!" she instructs, spreading her arms wide to indicate the room at large as she's dragged off by Elvis.

This whole experience is becoming more surreal by the minute.

I take another swallow of my drink as I scope the room again, the liquid sliding down my throat a little easier this time. I'm feeling out of my element and the need for my bed is outweighing the need to party. I drain the contents of the plastic cup – may as well enjoy a little nightcap before I leave - and pull out my cell to call a cab.

As I turn towards the door I don't see the puddle of beer on the floor and my feet skid out from underneath me.

I'm about to eat the ground in spectacular style when strong hands break my fall. Strong, *green* hands. I look up into a pair of chocolate brown eyes surrounded by a beautifully sculpted face which the green paint does nothing to disguise.

For a moment, it feels like we're suspended in time as I lose myself in the heat of his hands on my waist, his thumbs lingering just below my breasts and I can almost hear the *zap* of attraction that crackles in the air between us.

Before I can make sense of my overwhelming reaction, a pair

of sensual lips come crashing down against my own and I'm being kissed senseless by none other than Shrek. And, by God, Shrek is a good kisser!

It takes me a full minute to realize that not only am I enjoying the kiss, I'm also kissing him back. At some point my hands have tangled in his thick, dark hair as his tongue dances with mine. His mouth is making my whole body sing, making me want things.

Dirty things.

Filthy things.

Reality comes crashing down on me as I remember where we are and what I'm allowing him to do to me. I wrench myself out of his arms, which is no mean feat considering the size of him. He's a mountain of a man and it seems his costume choice fits him in more ways than one.

"Get your fucking hands off me!" I'm breathing heavily as I give him my best death stare – the one that normally makes men turn and run in the opposite direction.

I'm not sure why I'm so angry. Or so turned on.

My stare doesn't have any effect on Shrek and he doesn't move, looking a little shaken himself as he holds his hands up in the universal sign of surrender.

"Whilst I appreciate your help, I would've appreciated it more if you'd kept your tongue in your own mouth!"

I turn on my heel, without mishap this time, and march toward the door. As I leave, I am definitely not thinking about the feel of his mouth on mine or the annoying throb between my legs.

Nope, not thinking about it at all.

JAKE

Shit!

I watch as my blonde bombshell walks away, her back straight and her rounded ass swaying, making her skirt swish around her long legs. There's no way she can know that the feel of her soft curves against me has caused a reaction that hasn't occurred for months.

My dick went from zero to locked and loaded in two seconds flat and I couldn't help myself. Kissing her in that moment seemed as natural as taking my next breath. Those full red lips were begging for my mouth and I can't help but wonder how they'd feel wrapped around my now throbbing cock. Just the thought robs me of breath.

The white dress did nothing to disguise her hourglass figure and magnificent tits. Dear God, I was so capable in that moment I could've lifted her dress, slid her panties aside and buried myself in her heat right there and then!

My reaction is even more surprising because she's the exact opposite of my usual type of woman. I've always gone for blonde and tanned – or I did until my libido decided to go into early retirement six months ago.

I have no idea what her hair color is underneath the wig she was wearing but her lush curves are a direct contrast to my usual tastes, in the most delectable way.

I discreetly adjust the pants of my outfit and wonder again at the physical reaction she's just re-kindled. Who is this woman that's given my body a new lease of life? The urgency of that question diverts the blood from my dick back to my brain and I take off after her.

I head out the door and down the path in time to see a cab pulling away with my blonde bombshell in the back, her vivid green eyes looking back at me through the rear windscreen as the cab disappears into the night. Shit!

I go back inside, speaking to a few of the guests to see if anyone knows who she is, but no one remembers her. It's like she's a ghost – here one minute and gone the next. The only reminder of her is the twitch of my previously dormant cock when I remember her soft body against mine as we kissed.

Six months is a long time for a man to be dead from the waist down. In that time, I've gone from having an impressive one-eyed monster with a voracious appetite for pussy to a pathetic slow-worm with an inferiority complex.

I know it's my punishment for my man-ho ways after Monica and I split. That woman has done a number on me and I'm not sure I'll ever recover from her betrayal. I'll certainly never trust another woman again. I'd loved her, was going to marry her, believed she was having our baby.

All lies.

What a fucking gullible fool!

I fell for Monica the first time I saw her. She was beautiful, blonde and I wanted her. She was my first lover and I fell for her hard and deep. The feeling seemed to be mutual because she was on top of me in my bed the very same day, giving me an education in the ways of a woman's body.

Things were good for a while, we got along well and seemed to have similar tastes and outlooks on life. We'd been together for six months when she told me she was pregnant and the news had come as a complete surprise as she'd told me she was on birth control.

Once the shock wore off I quickly came around to the idea of being a daddy and was even more excited when her belly started to grow with our baby. Asking her to marry me had seemed like the next step – call me old-fashioned but I wanted our baby to have my name.

Then it had all gone to shit.

I came home early from training one afternoon and found her fucking another man in our bed. Caught in the act. No way she could deny that one. There's nothing like the pain of seeing your pregnant fiancée grinding away on another man's cock. Or being told that the child you thought was yours isn't - that the real father is the man whose cock she was grinding on. She took great pleasure in screaming that little nugget of information at me as I threw them both out.

She also told me in no uncertain terms that she'd never loved me and how I'd never satisfied her – in and out of bed. She'd just liked the attention being with a pro football player had brought her. The effect of those words was devastating and how I kept my fists to myself I'll never know. Part of me knew even then, with the fury running through my bloodstream, that if I hadn't I'd be in a jail cell somewhere and she would have won.

So, instead, I smashed up the bed until it was nothing but firewood and moved to a new apartment the next day. I couldn't stay there with the smell of their sex and deceit hanging in the air.

Then I went on the biggest bender imaginable, trying to lose the pain of her rejection at the bottom of a crate of beer and a different blonde every other night. Always blonde, each one a punishing reminder of her betrayal, a reminder never to give my heart over to any woman to be trampled on again.

I was upfront – no strings and no promises of commitment. Just sex, plain and simple, with no emotions at risk. I made sure I always used protection – no burying the bone unless I was wearing a cock-sock. No chance of another woman telling me I'd gotten her pregnant.

That arrangement was working fine, my only priorities getting drunk and getting laid, until six months ago when Puff the One-Eyed Dragon had stopped…puffing.

Despite a reputation I know I've earned in the last year, I haven't been near a woman for the last six months of it. The only good thing I can say about having a defective dick is that it's broken the self-destructive cycle I was on. I can admit now that I fucked up. I'm not proud of my six-month knee-jerk reaction to losing Monica and the only person it damaged in the long run was me.

My best friend, Tyler, has been there for me. He knew I was licking my wounds from Monica's betrayal, but he didn't push. He just waited in the background like a good friend until I was ready to spill my guts and was there for me the night I finally did.

I'm glad things have worked out for him and his girl, Jenna. He deserves to be happy and she seems like a genuinely sweet girl. It's obvious they're madly in love and it's good to see my friend with the real deal.

But pleased as I am for them, love is for other people now. I have no need for it.

Tonight, though, a blonde bombshell has unexpectedly brought my body back to life. Something about her has unlocked a psychological block and I need to find her.

I just don't know where to start.

Printed in Great Britain
by Amazon